# TRAIL OF LEAD

After the Baxter Springs bank is robbed, a bloody shootout between the thieves and the town's lawmen leaves only one bandit alive — Charlie Weston, who has escaped with the haul. Marshal Pete Baker and Deputy Joe Flaherty, already under threat of losing their badges, strike a bargain with Mayor Dell: they will track down Weston and the money within two months. If they fail, they'll resign. As Weston falls in with a wagon train heading west, the pursuit begins . . .

# MIKE DEANE

◆

# TRAIL OF LEAD

*Complete and Unabridged*

# LINFORD
*Leicester*

First published in Great Britain in 2019 by
Robert Hale
an imprint of The Crowood Press
Wiltshire

First Linford Edition
published 2023
by arrangement with The Crowood Press
Wiltshire

*A catalogue record for this book is available
from the British Library.*

ISBN 978–1–4448–4885–4

Published by
Ulverscroft Limited
Anstey, Leicestershire

Printed and bound in Great Britain by
TJ Books Ltd., Padstow, Cornwall

This book is printed on acid-free paper

*To all my girls*

# 1

Pete Baker and Joe Flaherty stalked down Main Street, Baxter Springs. Pete was on edge and Joe had finally given up trying to calm him. 'He's going to get rid of us,' Pete muttered. 'I'm sure of it. He has his own man lined up, that son of a —'

'He can't do that,' Joe interrupted. 'You've done a great job as marshal.'

'Thanks.' Pete glanced at his friend. 'And you've been a great deputy. But I don't think that counts for much with Mayor Dell.'

Joe didn't challenge Pete this time; he knew that there was no point. What Pete said could be true. He'd been marshal for two years now and he was doing as good a job as anyone could in a town as wild as Baxter Springs. But, he realised, if the mayor wanted to bring in his own man, there wasn't much he could do about it.

The job didn't mean as much to Joe, Pete knew. Joe was a Texan and could always ride back down the trail to the family ranch if necessary, whereas he, on the other hand, had made his life in Baxter Springs. He had Dorothy, a beautiful and loving wife, and three-month-old Tom. Being marshal helped support his family; it was an important source of income. His only source of income, in fact.

They strode along the wooden boardwalk until they reached the town hall and walked straight in. They were beckoned into the mayor's office. He offered them seats, smiling his nauseatingly obsequious smile at them as they entered. Mayor Dell sat behind an imposing oak desk which, Pete knew from his few dealings with him, Dell thought gave him an air of separation from the stream of commoners he dealt with on a daily basis. Pete felt like running around that desk and planting a fist in Dell's face. 'Welcome, men.' Dell's large bushy moustache moved up

2

and down as he spoke.

Pete was very much his own man and it was this trait that he knew caused Dell most frustration. He didn't feel the need to fill the mayor in on every little detail of his work. He simply believed that it was none of his business, just as he hadn't burdened the previous mayor with the minutiae of the job either. Pete would never make a politician, he knew that for sure, but he now realised that he might have to temper his stubbornness or it could cost him his job.

'You're probably wondering why I called you here,' Dell said.

'Let's not drag this out any longer than necessary,' Pete replied. Out of the corner of his eye he saw Joe cast a worried glance in his direction.

'What do you mean, Marshal?' Dell's voice was as sweet as molasses.

'Stop fooling around and get to the point, Mayor.' Pete was unable to play the game that he was sure Dell wanted him to play. The very injustice of the situation: the imminent removal of his job, his livelihood, his means of survival depending on the whim of a man like Dell was almost too much to bear. He wanted to get this over with quickly.

Dell arched an eyebrow and beckoned with his hand for Pete to continue with what he had to say.

'You're firing us, aren't you?'

His words hung over the room like a pall. Everything was now out in the open. He'd said what was on his mind. Joe shifted in his chair and shuffled his feet nervously, his hard-soled boots scraping the floorboards. Dell wore a smirk on his face.

'Come on, Joe,' Pete said, 'I don't want to stay where I'm not wanted.'

He got to his feet. Joe, too, stood, but Dell halted them before they could make for the door. 'Not so fast, boys. I didn't give you permission to leave.'

Pete felt his temper flare. He was about to tell Dell where he could shove his permission when he felt Joe's hand on his shoulder. He eyed his deputy's face and saw his look of concern. Concern that

4

he might say or do something that might have serious consequences. Even more serious than the loss of gainful employment. He would hold his tongue, for now at least. Whatever he felt about losing his job, spending a night, or two, in jail was not part of his plan.

'I didn't call you here to fire you,' Dell said, unable to hide the smugness in his voice, 'although after that little performance I might change my mind.'

Pete stared dead into the eyes of the mayor until Dell looked away.

'I know this is a tough town to control,' Dell said. 'Cattlemen bring money but also trouble. But the bottom line is that we need the cattle business. We'd be broke without it.'

Dell spoke the truth. Pete was the one who had to deal with the violent, drunk and randy cowboys and the chaos they brought with them each time a herd was driven to the town railheads. The saloons, hotels, brothels, whores, stores; all were dependent on the cowboys and their money.

'I don't know why you thought I was going to fire you,' Dell added. 'I think you're doing a good job.'

Something in Dell's voice prevented Pete from believing him completely.

'But . . .' Pete uttered. He left the rest of the sentence unfinished.

'Exactly,' Dell replied. 'But . . .' He let the word hang there for a moment before continuing. 'We need to get more money in taxes,' he said, speaking quickly to hide the quaver in his voice. 'I was thinking of bringing someone in to help you. Someone the businesses couldn't say no to.'

Pete let Dell's words settle like stones dropping to the bottom of the riverbed. Collecting fines and taxes was his least favourite part of the job, so any help in that regard would be welcome. If that was what Dell truly had in mind.

'Who were you thinking of?' Pete asked.

'Evan Taylor.'

'Evan Taylor? You sure?' Pete's reasoned tone of voice hid his incredulity at Dell's suggestion. Taylor was a thug and a gunsmith. During the previous cattle season, Taylor had raised some hell in the town, beat up a couple of whores and shot up Carley's General Store. In the end Pete and Joe gave him the option of either leaving Baxter Springs for good or spending some time in the town jail. Wisely, Taylor chose the first option. But now he was back, and with the mayor's blessing, it seemed.

'I'm not sure I could bear the sight of that thug wearing a shield,' Pete said.

'Well, I think he could do a good job for us and . . .' Dell raised his hand to stop Pete from interrupting, '. . . ultimately, the money collected from businesses goes to pay your salary. Just think about that, Pete.'

Dell didn't need to elaborate any further; it was clear to Pete what he was getting at.

'This has already been decided, hasn't it?'

Dell was silent.

'If I don't agree to this, Taylor will take over as marshal anyway.'

Dell didn't respond.

'Well?' Pete asked forcefully. He leaned forward in his chair, narrowing the distance between them.

'Now, Pete,' Dell said in a faltering voice, 'the reason I brought you here was so we could talk about this.'

'And if I say no?'

The mayor took his time, trying desperately to regain his composure. Finally, he said, 'You have a wife, Pete. And a baby . . .'

'I see,' Pete replied. 'So that's the way it's going to be.'

He sat back in his chair. He burned inside with frustration and anger. He loved being marshal of Baxter Springs and drew great satisfaction from trying to manage the town as best he could. He'd become part of the community and that had given him a sense of worth. And, most importantly, he earned a good living for himself and his family. And that had to be the foremost concern in his mind. Ultimately, he couldn't afford to put that living in undue jeopardy.

'Joe stays as my deputy, all right?' was all he said, trying to hide the defeat in his voice.

'I'm glad we've come to an agreement.' Dell rose and reached his hand across the table. It remained hanging in the air, untouched, as Pete and Joe walked out the door.

# 2

Five men rode toward the outskirts of town. Charlie Weston drew his overcoat tighter around him and pulled his hat down lower over his eyes. The four men with him did the same. It wasn't cold, or wet; they weren't dressed in these heavy coats with high collars for any other reason than to conceal their identities and the weapons they carried.

Weston chewed on an unlit thick cigar, tense but not nervous. He'd been through this many times before over the last few years, although not with this band. He found it more and more difficult to find reliable and loyal gunmen. If all went well, this would be the last time he'd have to draw his Colt in anger. He was eager for it all to end. He found it harder to keep going now. The lifespan of an outlaw was only so long, and he felt that his luck might be coming to an end. That was one reason why this job was so important. He had plans, and this payout should allow him to make them real. The town was quiet as they rode along the street. The five men passed unnoticed; if anybody saw them, they'd be mistaken for cowmen or drovers.

Weston reined in outside the bank. The men dismounted and tied their horses to the hitching rail. Not a word passed between them; they knew their roles. Two men fanned out and covered the approaches to the clapboard building. The other two followed Weston.

He fought to control his breathing as he approached the front door. His nerve endings tingled with excitement. He did not feel any fear. What had he left to fear, anyway? He had nothing to lose, nobody waiting for him. He just had to look after himself, and this was his way of doing just that.

Weston pushed open the front door and entered the bank, closely followed by one of his men, a grizzled old outlaw named Stewart. The other man stayed outside to make sure that nobody

11

else followed them in. There were just two staff, a clerk and a cashier, sitting behind a wooden counter. Weston didn't go to the desk but stopped and warmed his hands at the stove placed just inside the door. Instead, he watched Stewart approach the clerk.

'Can you change this for me, friend?' Stewart growled as he slid a ten-dollar bill across the polished counter. The clerk reached for the bill but stopped midway as the steel barrel of Stewart's revolver pressed against his temple. The cashier leaped to his feet to help his colleague, instinct trumping restraint.

'I wouldn't do that,' snarled Weston from behind his cigar. The cashier was halted by the sound of the hammer of Weston's gun being drawn back. 'I said stop, feller. Or I *will* blast your head off.'

The tone of Weston's voice left the cashier in no doubt that he meant what he said.

'Let's not waste any time,' Weston said forcefully. His men outside would keep watch but there was always the danger that a curious lawman would show up and note the muffled figures outside the town's only bank and grow suspicious. He had to expedite matters and, from experience, he knew that brutality was often the best way of shocking people into action.

The two bank staff stared at him, either unwilling or unable to move. Weston nodded almost imperceptibly to Stewart. The thug's right arm flashed across the desk, striking the clerk's face with the butt of his Colt.

Weston grabbed the cashier by the shoulder. He shoved him toward the open bank vault, the man half stumbling on his way, clearly shocked by what he'd seen happen to his colleague. The clerk now lay on the floor, blood seeping from the wound on his face, his low moans rolling around the building. Weston shoved the cashier into the vault and flung him a grain sack he'd concealed in his coat. 'Be quick!' he barked.

The cashier began to fill the sack with gold and silver coins, the sounds from the currency temporarily drowning out the lowing from his injured friend. He worked methodically while, outside the vault, Stewart hauled the clerk to his feet and tried to shake the grogginess from him.

'Where's the paper money?' he demanded. The clerk slumped back to his knees, a glazed expression on his face. Stewart raised his gun again, ready to strike him once more.

'In the box,' the cashier shouted from inside the vault, his voice shrill with panic and fright. He wasn't sure that he could bear the sight or sound of any more violence. Wasn't sure if he could endure the sickening, sharp crack of gun striking bone. Wasn't sure he could listen to any more primal, animal sounds of aggression and pain. His hand shook as he pointed to a large tin container inside the vault.

Stewart came into the vault and stuffed the contents of the box — currency, bonds, bank notes and sheets of revenue stamps — into another sack. Weston stepped out of the vault, his grain sack bulging. Stewart grabbed the clerk and dragged him roughly across the floor toward the vault. He flung him inside.

'Stay in there,' Weston said sinisterly, 'if you know what's good for you.'

Weston glanced at his fob watch. He reckoned they had been in the bank for a total of eight minutes.

★ ★ ★

Darkness enveloped the two bank staff as the vault door slammed shut. Relief flooded through Ralph, the cashier. Relief that the raiders had gone, that he wouldn't be hurt, and that it was his colleague who had suffered from their violence and not him. They could be in the vault for hours, he realised in an abstract sort of way, as if it was of no great concern to him. All he need do was just wait until someone let them out and then he'd go about his day as normal.

But Andy couldn't be ignored. The cashier lay at his feet, the sounds of his hurt filling the small room. Ralph knelt beside him. He couldn't see Andy's wound in the darkness, for which he was grateful. He didn't know what to say to his friend, how to reassure him. As he dredged his mind for suitable words, he noticed a thin sliver of light entering the vault from around the door frame. Jammed in it was a loose coin, preventing it from closing fully.

'Back in a minute,' Ralph muttered to his stricken colleague as he shoved at the vault door. It gave a little. At one forceful push with all of his body weight the door opened and he was out. The bank was empty, but through the bank's large glass window he saw the outlaws disappearing down the street.

He burst out the front door and shouted at the top of his voice: 'Robbed! We've been robbed!' He pointed down the street at the group of riders heading out of town and frantically called out again for help.

\* \* \*

Pete was silent as he walked away from the mayor's office with Joe.

'What're you thinking, Marshal?' Joe asked.

'You know you don't have to call me that. Pete will do just fine.'

'Well, whatever I call you, the question's the same. What d'you think of what just happened in there?'

'I think he's trying to get rid of us, no matter what he says. Well, get rid of me at least. But he doesn't have the courage to do it like a man.'

'I think it's because he knows that he doesn't have the support. If he got rid of you all the businessmen would be furious. He'd get run out of town.'

'I'm not so sure. He wants Evan Taylor in as marshal, that's for sure. I don't know why, but that's the road he's headed down and I'm not sure there's much I can do about it. He is the mayor, after all.'

Pete was silent for a moment and then added, 'Let's get some breakfast. Things might seem a little straighter after a cup of coffee and some food.'

A cry pierced the air, cutting through their worries about the mayor and wiping out their plans to fill their bellies. 'What was that?' Joe asked.

Pete had already broken into a run and half-turned to shout, 'Somebody's just robbed the bank by the sounds of it!'

They rushed to their horses, mounted up and rode in the direction the distraught cashier was pointing, their horses' hoofs kicking up dust from the dry ground as they went.

They rode out on the cattle trail, that broad worn sweep of ground gouged into the soil outside Baxter Springs by the beasts that gave the town life.

The outlaws couldn't be that far ahead, Pete knew. He felt a fire burning within, fuelling a drive to catch the men who dared rob the bank in his town. This was the first bank robbery since he'd become marshal and he felt a personal hurt at the crime. And, though he wouldn't admit it, or maybe even realise it, his meeting with the mayor spurred him on also. This pursuit gave him something to focus on, and prove that he was a good lawman.

Joe gradually fell behind, his mount unable to match Pete's. Pete disappeared around a sweeping curve in the trail and Joe lost him from sight, the dust kicked up by his horse blocking his view. He fought to get more from his mount to try and gain some ground, but with no success. Then he heard a sound that sent a chill down his spine; the sound of gun-shots.

Joe drew his Colt and pulled back the hammer. He rounded the curve in the trail, nerves jangling, wary of what might lie ahead. He heard gunfire once more and felt a bullet whistle past his ear. He pulled back on the reins, anxious not to ride into an ambush. He ducked his head low behind his horse's neck for cover. As he did so, he heard a shout from his left.

'Joe,' Pete called, 'get over here!' Pete had dismounted and lay crouched in a depression behind a small hillock off to the side of the trail.

A shot cracked the air again and once

more Joe heard the whistle of a bullet as it passed close by, the sound of death seeking him out. He was an easy target sitting in the middle of the trail like this; he had to get under cover.

Pete poked his head over the top of the ridge and fired off two quick shots at some target in the distance. Joe took his chance, quickly dismounted and dashed over to where Pete lay. His horse turned tail and fled back toward Baxter Springs.

'They were waiting for me,' Pete panted. 'Dry-gulched me.'

'You hit?' Joe asked.

Pete shook his head.

'Where they firing from?' Joe shouted above the sound of the gunfire.

'Behind a ditch just up the way a little. Five of them. Just saw the barrel of a Winchester poking out as I came round the bend. Took cover just in time.'

'Bless your sight, Pete, I didn't see a thing. I'd have ridden straight into them.'

'That was their plan.'

The shooting stopped momentarily and Pete used the opportunity to take a quick look over the top of their cover. He dropped back down just as quickly. 'They're going to try and roust us out,' he said. 'They've got us outnumbered, but I've never known an outlaw to have more stomach for a fight than you or me.'

Joe nodded in agreement.

'They'll probably send two fellers around our side, try to outflank us, under covering fire from the other three. That's what I'd do anyway. They'll try to keep our heads down until the other jiggers are close enough to blow our heads off. But we'll be ready for them,' he said with grim determination.

'Just like the war again,' Joe said quietly.

Pete nodded. He quickly described his plan of action to Joe. 'It's risky,' he said when he had finished. 'But right now it doesn't seem as if we've got any other choice.'

★ ★ ★

Weston finished giving his instructions to his men. He was furious that they hadn't killed the marshal outright but Travers had fired too early. To make matters worse, they'd also failed to hit the deputy. Now, instead of being home free they were stuck in a shoot-out in the middle of the plain. This couldn't continue, Weston knew. There might be a posse on the way from the town, hungry for blood. His blood. Even in a place like Baxter Springs, a full-scale gun-party couldn't continue indefinitely without attracting some measure of attention. It was time to resolve this impasse, and quickly.

'Travers and Collier,' he called.

The pair looked at him reluctantly, aware from his tone of voice that they wouldn't like what he had in mind.

'You two fan out and come around the sides of that hillock. We'll cover you. And,' he said pointedly at Travers, 'make sure you don't miss this time.'

'Why us?' Travers protested. 'Why don't you go if you're so worried we won't do it right?' Anger welled within Weston once more. He hated Travers now, his emotion was that strong. Hated them all, in fact. If he'd thought that he could've pulled off the robbery by himself, he would have; it would have been worth the risk instead of having to stare at the sullen face of this idiot. The face of a man who just wanted to collect easy money, who didn't want to work or take orders.

'Because I said so,' Weston replied, slowly, as if he were speaking to a child. He had to use all his strength to keep his frustration in check.

'So what?' Travers rasped.

A single shot rang out and Travers clutched at his chest. The others ducked for cover, all except Weston and Stewart. Smoke drifted from the barrel of Stewart's Colt and dissipated slowly into the late-morning air.

'Any more questions?' Weston asked.

There were none.

'Donnachie, you take Travers' place.'

This time there were no arguments.

Donnachie and Collier stepped over the dying form of Travers as they left the cover of the ditch. Seconds later, Stewart and Weston lay down covering fire.

★ ★ ★

Joe was about to jump into action when the shot that killed Travers echoed. Pete grabbed him by his shirtfront to steady him and gestured for him to wait a moment.

'What's happening?' Joe mouthed.

Pete wasn't sure, but he knew he couldn't afford to betray his plan too early. If it didn't come off, they'd be going home as corpses, of that he had no doubt. He had no illusions about the savagery of gunfights. He'd witnessed the barbarity and brutishness they brought out in people and seen too much of their aftermath. Gunfights unleashed base instinct, the instinct for survival, to live, even if it was at the expense of another person. He'd never previously had any fear of slaughter.

But things were different, now.

*Must stay alive. For them.*

He thought of Dorothy and little Tom back in the Ranchers' Saloon. Dorothy's father, Cal, owned the business and Dorothy helped him run it. Did they even know that he was out here, his life hanging by a thread? They'd be wondering why he hadn't come home for breakfast, why he hadn't checked in. Maybe they wouldn't be wondering at all. Word of the bank robbery would spread. They'd know, all right. He couldn't be farther from them now, he thought. But there was only one way to get back there. Kill or be killed. It was the law of this land.

He took a deep breath. There was still no firing from the ditch. Maybe he'd been wrong? Maybe the outlaws were crawling toward them even now, Bowie knives drawn, ready to slit their throats? This thought sent a chill through him, despite the growing heat.

He tensed his body, ready to crawl around the side of the hillock to see the lie of the land. He knew that he might be offering himself as an easy target. But he also knew that he couldn't just lie there doing nothing, waiting for death's cold embrace. He dropped onto his belly and removed his hat. He turned to Joe and indicated that he must not follow him.

He crawled forward on his elbows. It was only a few feet to a spot where he could peer round a small undulation and get a view of the plain. They wouldn't be expecting him to appear there, he reckoned, away from the main cover of the hillock. And, if the worst came to the worst and he was seen and fired upon, maybe even killed, at least he would have given Joe some warning.

He lay flat against the dry, dusty ground, his nose pressed against the dirt. Sweat spilled down his face. The ridge was just high enough to hide him but it tapered away until it became one with the plain. He brought his revolver up from his hip and pulled back the hammer, ready to fire. He knew he'd be a sitting duck if spotted; one gun against five, as far as he knew, with very little cover. One of those bullets was bound to find its target. But the other option, to wait for death to come around the hill and take them, was no option for Pete Baker. He wasn't going to allow that to happen.

He tensed, ready to stick his head into the open. 'Now or never, Pete,' he muttered, sounding braver than he felt. His thoughts were interrupted by a sudden fusillade of shots that filled the air and the impact of bullets into the hillock.

Joe wasn't sure what to do. Pete's plan hadn't involved him being yards away with his nose buried in dirt when the lead started flying. To his left, he saw Pete trying to make himself as small as possible to avoid getting hit. He heard bullets singing overhead as well as thudding into the hillock and the ground all around him. But Pete didn't seem to have been hit. They mustn't have seen him, he concluded. They weren't firing at him, either. This must be their covering fire for the men who were going to outflank them.

'Pete!' he roared, straining to be heard above the din. 'They're not firing at you, they haven't seen you!' Joe saw Pete rise onto his haunches. He looked about for a moment before shouting to Joe: 'Do it!'

Joe understood immediately and pressed his back hard against the hillock. Its summit was just above his head. Joe removed his hat and in one smooth move landed it on top of the ridge. Before it landed, he was rolling away to his right.

He heard lead being emptied into his hat, as though the robbers' fire concentrated on that one point. He regretted the loss of that hat, a gift from his mother. His Colt ready, he looked across at Pete and received a definite nod. It was time.

Both Pete and Joe broke cover at the same time, guns blazing. As they rose up they charged almost directly into Collier and Donnachie. The outlaws' expressions changed from shocked surprise to terror as they realised they were now easy targets. Joe and Pete cut them down. Pete was so close he could smell the stale sweat that permeated the outlaws' bodies as they fell dead. Now there were just those behind the ditch.

Bullets chased their feet, kicking up dust as they ran. Pete didn't bother crouching low, he just ran as hard as he could toward the low ditch. He saw the man firing at him, an old grizzled feller with his hat pulled low and the barrel of his Winchester tracking him. Yet Pete moved fast and closed the distance between them quickly. He couldn't see the other gang members, and presumed that they were somewhere close by. He fired a couple of shots quickly at the ditch, forcing the outlaw to duck for cover. The barrel of the rifle reappeared, just feet away. He fired his Colt but the bullet missed and struck the ground directly in front of the outlaw. His gun clicked empty: he was a sitting duck.

Time lengthened as Pete clearly saw the features of the man who was preparing to kill him; the sun-bronzed face, beaten harshly by the wind, the lines like furrows that creased his forehead. And there was nothing Pete could do about it; he was powerless, destined to run into the ball of lead that would travel toward him at a ferocious speed and rip through his shirt and skin and make a mess of his internal organs, tearing them beyond repair and rendering the shiny marshal's badge on his chest no more useful than a toy little Tom might play with. Pete's mouth gaped open when he heard the gunshot. A shout, a primeval roar, forced itself from his lungs as if competing with the noise of the very thing destined to kill him. He felt nothing, surprised that the impact of something that could take so much from him, take everything from him, didn't cause more pain. Didn't strike him like a bolt of lightning, dissolving him on the spot. His legs kept moving, his cry kept sounding, filling him from within, blocking out all external sensations, wrapping him in a cocoon of black noise until he found himself standing over the prone body of the grizzled outlaw, blood seeping from the man's temple.

He stopped, stunned and confused.

Unable to comprehend what had just happened.

'Pete!' Joe called.

Pete stood still, dazed, gazing foolishly at the dead man at his feet. He lifted his head and looked across at Joe.

'I got him, Pete,' Joe said, holding up his smoking revolver. 'I got him.'

# 3

Pete and Joe sat around Dorothy's kitchen table in the back of the Ranchers' Saloon. Pete's hands shook as he raised a mug of coffee to his lips. Dorothy stood by the table, too restless to sit. Pete listened to Joe as yet again he related the events of the day.

'So you got the money back?' she asked.

Pete didn't answer. At last, Joe shook his head. 'Afraid not. One of the jiggers got away. Saw his tracks heading cross-country. He was long gone by the time the shooting finished. Might even have been gone before the shooting started.'

'And he had all the money from the bank?'

'Guess so.'

There was silence around the table.

'This is the end,' Pete said wearily.

'What d'you mean?' she asked.

'Dell. He'll definitely get rid of us now.'

'What?' she said, surprise evident in her voice. 'Banks get robbed all the time and marshals don't lose their jobs over it. Surely he can't fire you just for this.'

Pete didn't reply. He couldn't be sure what he might say. He left it to Joe to tell her about the meeting they'd had with the mayor that morning.

'So what if he fires you?' Dorothy said defiantly after Joe finished.

'So what?' A little fire returned to Pete's voice. 'What about our plans?' he asked, the cadence of his voice rising. 'What about the homestead we were going to buy? If I lose my job, it's just not possible.'

The sound of boots on the wooden floor of the kitchen interrupted him.

Paul Henry, one of the lawmen who worked with Pete and Joe, entered.

'Sorry to disturb you, ma'am,' Paul said, nodding toward Dorothy. 'But the mayor wants to see you fellers,' he said, looking at Pete and Joe.

'Thanks, Paul,' Pete said.

Paul hastily withdrew. 'This is it,' Pete said. He rose slowly and picked his hat up from the table. 'We'd better —' The words died in his throat as he felt the sharp sting of a slap across his cheek. He staggered back a step, stunned by the sudden blow. He hadn't seen it coming; Dorothy had lashed out like a rattlesnake.

'I'll . . .' Joe stammered as he made for the door.

'You stay right there, Joe Flaherty,' Dorothy shouted, 'unless you want some as well.'

'No, ma'am, I mean, yes, ma'am. I mean . . .' He collapsed into his chair.

Dorothy stood, her cheeks flushed. 'I don't know what's happening to you today, Pete Baker, but I do know for sure that the man I married wouldn't give up something he loved so easily.' Pete opened his mouth to reply but her glare quieted him. 'I'm here in the saloon, minding little Tom and helping my father. What would you say if I told you I was giving it all up just because some drunk made my life difficult? You wouldn't let me, that's what, because you know I love it here. Heck, even when we *do* move out to our farm, I'll be back here helping out. I know you love being the marshal here, Pete, and if Mayor Dell is going to take that away from you, then he will. But you're certainly not going to roll over to have your belly kicked. You're not going to say "thank you very much" when he takes the badge from your shirt. I know a good wife would tell her husband to do whatever he feels is right, that if he wanted to leave his job that she'd support him, no matter what. Well, that's a load of bull! If you go in there and fight for what you love doing, then I'll support you, if not . . .'

She left the sentence unfinished.

Pete exhaled slowly. He realised he'd been holding his breath. Dorothy's words hung in the air like smoke after a gunshot. He stared up at her. He didn't feel embarrassment at being castigated in front of Joe; all he could feel was love for the beautiful woman before him, the mother of his child. She was right, of course, like she always was; even when she wasn't. Something had happened to him out on the plain, he'd felt his own mortality like never before. Discovered that he had more to lose than he ever realised. Baby Tom's arrival had changed something within him. And the extra responsibility weighed on his shoulders.

*His family.*

That phrase rang around his head. That's what he was scared of losing. Scared of leaving little Tom without a father; scared of not having those years ahead with his son that he hoped to enjoy.

But he couldn't hide from reality. For the present, at least, he was still the marshal of Baxter Springs, and he had to act like it. He had to fight for his job and for his own self-respect, if not for any other reason. So he could hold his head high when he came back to his wife and child and call himself the head of his family.

He rose from his seat without saying a word and pulled Dorothy close to him.

She resisted for a moment, but when she felt the force of his kiss, she relaxed gladly.

\* \* \*

Once more they sat in Dell's office. This time, however, there was someone else in the room: Evan Taylor, standing behind the mayor's seat.

'What happened this morning?' Dell asked. He smiled as a hungry cat might at a lame mouse.

'You know well what happened, Mayor,' Pete replied. 'The money was stolen from the bank and I all but got blasted to kingdom come for trying to get it back. But for Joe, here, I'd be worm food by now.'

'I understand your anger, Marshal, and I thank you for your efforts, but you didn't get the money back, did you? Any of it? Not one cent?'

He imagined the satisfying feeling of his knuckles connecting with Dell's fatty mouth, permanently knocking the sneer from his face. He fought to contain his anger.

'We never had a chance of recovering that money,' he said. 'And the men we killed would never have seen any of it either. Whoever was behind this job wasn't going to share the cash. The others were just tools to be used to get what he wanted and then to be thrown away when he was finished with them. It just happened that we saved him from doing the worst of the dirty work.'

Perversely, Pete had a grudging respect for the outlaw. He wasn't beholden to anybody, had taken what he wanted and gotten away scot-free. Not like him, an upstanding citizen dependent on the whims of a mayor who made him feel physically nauseous.

'We'll get the money back, or at least catch the thieves,' Pete said suddenly. Out of the corner of his eye he noticed Joe's head turn, his eyes open wide, questioning. Pete kept staring at the mayor.

Dell's face also registered surprise but he quickly hid it with the same insincere smile.

'Will you, now?' he asked archly. 'I take it, then, that you must have some idea who committed the crime, is that correct? Or maybe you know where they're hiding out?'

Pete just shook his head. 'Not a clue.'

Dell stared at him for a full ten seconds before bursting into laughter. 'You hear that, Evan?' he asked Taylor. 'Our marshal can smell stolen money. Sniff it out like a dog.'

Taylor just grunted. He hadn't moved from his position beside Dell's chair. He was like a silent sentry surveying all that was going on.

'You want to fire us, Dell,' Pete said, his voice even, but with a hard edge. He was going to fight, as Dorothy had implored him. He was going to turn this to his advantage, somehow. He just hoped he was going the right way about it. 'But I'm going to make you another offer.'

'You're going to make *me* an offer?' Dell said incredulously. 'I'm not sure you're in any position to do such a thing.

Do you know what damage a bank robbery will do to this town? The bank may pull out altogether. I expect someone from their headquarters in Leavenworth today to come and discuss the matter, and I'm not sure the outcome will be good for Baxter Springs.'

'That may be true, but what if me and Joe succeeded in finding that money or bringing in the robber? I'm pretty sure that would please the fellers from Leavenworth. And it would be a warning to anybody else planning to rob a bank here that they wouldn't get away with it.'

'I'm sure it would,' Dell replied, 'but, as I said earlier, how is that going to happen? We seem to be going round and round in circles here, Pete, without you making any sense.'

'Pay me and Joe our wages for the next two months; give us that time to find the money.' Pete saw that Dell was about to object, so he raised his hand. 'Hear me out, Mayor, give me a moment.' Dell nodded, his eyes screwed up, wary. 'Make Taylor the marshal while we're chasing the money. I know that's what you want to do anyway and this will give you the ideal opportunity. You can see if he's the right man for the job. If Joe and I don't succeed, then we'll go quietly, without a fight. And when the feller from Leavenworth calls, you can tell him you even have the marshal and his deputy on the job. He'll like the sound of that, and it might even buy you some time. That's my offer, Mayor.' Pete sat back in his chair and folded his arms.

Silence filled the room. All eyes were now turned expectantly toward Dell. He looked up at Taylor, as if seeking a sign from the big man.

Taylor shrugged his shoulders. 'Seems fine by me,' he mumbled. 'Way I see it, I become marshal and these jokers will be out of here after two months. It's a no-lose deal.'

Dell looked across at Pete. 'You've got a deal.' As they walked away from the town hall, Joe said, 'I hope you know what you're doing.'

'So do I, Joe. So do I . . .'

Weston woke early, the dawn just breaking over the prairie as he slid out from under his blanket. He was in the ruined remains of an old homestead that had burned during the war. Owner probably lying in a grave somewhere, his family too, like his own parents. He'd tried long enough to forget about what happened to them. These matters didn't concern him now, however; he sought the ruins to escape detection. He couldn't care less what had happened to the previous inhabitants, despite the similarities to the fate of his own family. Until now, he'd banished all thoughts of that time from his memory; it was as if it never happened. All he could think of now was how to avoid capture.

He thought of the previous day's debacle. He'd been lucky to escape. It was the closest he'd ever been to getting caught. It was fitting that this was his last job. It was as if fate was giving him a warning. He had the money beside him, close to his body. It was everything. It was his future. He rose to his feet and breathed in the morning air. It was important to keep moving. They were more than likely after him, searching for his tracks. He'd been careful, though. Left no evidence; well, as far as he could tell. There were no loose ends. Nothing to trip him up.

He tied the grain sacks either side of the saddle, making sure they were closed tight. There was no breakfast; food wasn't important to him this morning. He had things to do and, all going well, everything would be sorted by the end of the day. No, everything would definitely be in place by the end of the day. It had to be. The rest of his life was about to begin. He mounted up, the early morning sun beginning to wash the land with its soft light. He rode briskly away. Time to put his money to work.

# 4

*Two weeks later. Lawrence, Kansas*

Blood spattered the walls of the saloon. Two bodies lay on the floor, life seeping through the floorboards and onto the dry ground below. The door to the saloon hung open. The gunman had just disappeared through it, pursued by two men. This had been more than just another job for the gunman. More than the usual order that involved killing a couple of men. This time he had done it for himself.

His breath rasped in his throat, as if barbed wire were being forced down his gullet. His feet pounded the hard dirt as he ran into the night. His body ached, stretched to breaking point. But still he kept on going. He stole a glance over his shoulder but all he saw were the lights of the town.

His Colt .44 slapped against his thigh as he ran, its barrel still warm. Even though he was sweating profusely, a cold chill passed through him. The sounds of the chase carried to him on the wind. The sound of death. He changed direction, angling to his left, like a hunted rabbit. He felt lightheaded; running blind in the dark.

He stumbled once, falling in a heap in the dust, smashing his right knee into the hard ground. He scrambled to his feet, weaker now, his body responding more slowly. He stubbed his foot on a rock and fell forward, his hands clawing at the air as he tried to keep his balance. This time, when he fell, his head crashed against a stone.

The last thing he saw before passing out was a bearded face staring at him down the barrel of a Winchester.

\* \* \*

He opened his eyes slowly, gradually allowing daylight to seep into his aching head. His body jolted and his head hit off something hard. He cursed loudly clutching his head in his hands.

'Looks like our guest is awake,' came a voice from somewhere. 'Give him some water, Betty.'

He heard sounds of scrambling and within moments a canteen was pressed to his lips. He drank thirstily, washing away the dust and pain and fear. Slowly, his head began to clear and he felt a little of his strength returning. The canteen was taken away and he propped himself up on his elbows, face to face with a woman wearing a gingham dress and a Poke bonnet. She smiled benignly on him. Then there was another great jolt and he was slammed down on his back once more. That's when he realised that they were moving.

He looked about. He was in a wagon, lying on its flat wooden floor. The woman had left. Maybe he'd imagined her? He wondered who she was. She couldn't be with Maxwell; he'd be dead by now if she was.

He wasn't wearing his coat and he frantically scoured the wagon until he realised that he'd been using it as a pillow.

He unfolded it and reached to an inside pocket. What he felt there reassured him and he allowed himself a smile. When he put his hand to his hip he discovered that his Colt was missing, however. He rose unsteadily to his feet, his back hunched over, the wagon roof too low to allow him to stand upright. 'Time to figure out what the hell is going on,' he muttered.

The covered wagon was not designed for comfort and he found himself dodging various household items as he tried to gain his feet. He staggered toward the daylight that streamed through the open end of the wagon. Sitting up there was the woman who had given him the water, beside what looked like the strong square back of a man. Weston's boots thumped on the floor as he moved so that the man heard his approach and turned to face him. He recognized the wagoner's bearded face immediately: the last thing he'd seen before he passed out.

'Come up and join us,' the bearded man said, his voice booming in the confines of the wagon. 'Bit of a tight squeeze,

I'm afraid.'

The woman moved over and Weston sat next to her. Pulling the wagon were two yoke of oxen, plodding along slowly and deliberately. Ahead were four more wagons, saddle horses and mules. As well as the wagons and the oxen pulling them, many more steers and cows wandered along the prairie.

'Welcome to our Prairie Schooner,' said the woman.

This was an emigrant train, it slowly dawned on Weston. He nodded in reply.

'Name's Chet Harrington,' said the broad-shouldered man, 'and this here is my wife, Betty, whom you've already met.'

'Howdy,' he growled in reply.

'If you're going to stay with us, you'll have to speak to McCann, the head man. He'll decide what's to become of you.'

Weston spoke little for the rest of the day as they meandered across the prairie, trying to get things straight in his head. As evening fell, the wagoners halted for the night and Weston helped them get their cattle settled. The other emigrants hadn't paid much attention to him during the day except for a few curious glances cast in his direction.

What would he say to them? Chet had saved his life but he knew nothing about him. Chet might just as quickly shoot him or leave him hanging from a branch if he learned of what he'd done and who he was. He resolved to play it by ear. If the worst came to the worst, he could steal a horse and make his escape. Even without his Colt, he was sure that he could fight his way out.

They settled to eat in the clearing formed by the circled wagons. A fire burned in the middle and the families ate by their wagons, in silence, weary from the day's travelling. Weston ate his meal with Chet and Betty. When they had finished the folks from the other wagons drew near and they all mingled and talked as they drank watery coffee. There were four wagons in all, he observed; a small train, he learned.

'These are all nice people,' Betty told

him, 'but they can be suspicious of outsiders.'

He nodded. He didn't know if Chet had told the others how he had found him. He would find out soon enough. Chet patted him on the shoulder as he got up. He walked away, leaving him with Betty. They would come for him soon, he knew.

The men gathered in a group. They stole glances at him out of the corner of their eyes as they talked amongst themselves. In the twilight, he found it difficult to make out how many there were in this group. Four wagons meant at least four men, and probably accompanying wives and children too. He assessed the situation as he had many over the years and thought the odds were in his favour; if it should come to it.

A figure emerged out of the gloom, the tip of his cigarette glowing in the darkness.'My name's McCann, Emmet McCann. How're ya doing, feller?'

He sized McCann up. Maybe fifty years old, give or take. Flecks of grey showed in his beard but he was in impressive physical condition.

'I'm in charge of this company and Chet's told me all he knows about you, which ain't much.' Weston didn't reply. 'Says he left camp last night to go into Lawrence to buy some supplies and ended up with a stray.' He stared. 'My only responsibility is to the folks in this wagon train. You could be a murderer as far as I know, waiting to slit everyone's throat.'

Three more shapes loomed behind McCann. He recognized one as Chet but not the other two. They didn't offer their names. They were wearing their gunbelts and all but Chet had their hands on their shooters. They moved closer and stood over him, trying to intimidate him, he imagined. He stayed sitting, sipping his coffee.

Chet spoke first: 'Seeing as it was me that found you, and the bad state you were in, I think I'm entitled to a few answers at least.'

'Fair enough,' Weston replied. He

looked Chet straight in the eyes and ignored the others. He owed Chet some explanation, even if it wasn't an entirely truthful one. If Chet hadn't found him — The alternative didn't bear thinking about.

'Ask away,' he said.

'What's your name? And why were you running away from those fellers like they were the hounds of hell?'

He drained the last of his coffee and rose slowly to his feet. His interrogators took a step back as he stood, all except Chet. He looked at each of them in turn. 'Name's Charlie Weston,' he said, 'and the first thing you should know is that I don't want no trouble. The reason I was running out of town last night when Chet found me was because I'd danced with the wrong lady in the dancehall. Her husband didn't take too kindly to that and decided to teach me a lesson. Had to go out through the window, couldn't get to my horse. That's the beginning and the end of it.' He met each of their gazes in turn until the men looked away.

They weren't going to get any more out of him, at least not for the moment.

'What d'ya think?' one of the men asked McCann. Weston sized him up. Smaller than the others, but wiry. Strong-looking. These were probably all family men, with children most likely, as well. They wouldn't take kindly to him if they thought he might cause danger to their group. Maybe he shouldn't have said that he'd danced with another man's wife. Maybe he should have told the truth.

'I don't know, Walt,' McCann replied.

'Well, I don't like the look of him,' the fourth man said. 'I don't believe a word he says. I can find out easily enough about him, Emmet. I've a brother living in Lawrence, remember? He'll let us know who this feller really is.'

'I'm not from Lawrence,' Weston replied. 'Just passing through when I got mixed up in that bother last night. Don't know anybody there.'

'Now, take it easy,' Chet soothed. 'Let's go back to your wagon, Frank, and talk about this.'

Weston now knew the names of the four men. Chet: broad, bearded, reasonable; Emmet: in charge, imposing; Walt: small and wiry. And Frank, who was staring at him with distaste.

Weston sat back on the ground and lit a cigarette. He could hear the men discussing in voices that were occasionally raised in exclamation. He couldn't tell if things were going in his favour and neither did he care.

They returned after a few minutes. Weston rose to his feet and walked in their direction in his long purposeful stride.

'Where are ye headed?' he asked. 'California? Oregon?'

'California,' McCann replied warily.

'Through Fort Laramie, right?'

McCann nodded.

'Any of you crossed the Platte before?'

He could tell by their silence that they hadn't.

'The question here is whether I should stick with you and not the other way around,' Weston said. 'I know this country like the back of my hand, every fording point, the best places to camp and I know what to do if Indians start harassing you.' He paused for a moment.

The wagoners remained quiet.

'So,' he said at last, 'I've decided. I'll stay. Today is your lucky day.'

He turned on his heel and headed back to his resting place, leaving the four men standing in silence.

'Welcome aboard,' Chet murmured eventually.

# 5

Dan Bogue could see all of the saloon as
he sipped his whisky. It was early evening
and beginning to fill with the usual flow
of cattle drovers, soiled doves and locals.
Bogue finished his drink and was about
to rise to leave when a man entered. He
wasn't the usual sort who frequented the
saloon: his clothes were too well cut, his
bearing superior to that of the average
drunken cowboy. Bogue knew immediately that this man had come looking for
him.

Bogue's hand slipped to his ornately
engraved Colt, sitting snugly in its holster. The well-dressed man crossed the
floor quickly, Bogue glaring at him as
he approached. Bogue guessed that he
was maybe in his sixties. Even though
his clothes were well made and refined
in appearance, his face bore the signs
of a life well lived. He now stood across
the table from Bogue, his broad frame

filling his vision. 'Dan Bogue?' he asked, his voice a deep bass.

'Maybe,' Bogue replied. 'Depends who's asking.'

This brought a smile to the man's lips. 'Name's Maxwell,' he replied. 'Bat Maxwell. And I know that you are Dan Bogue.'

Bogue eyed him. He shoved a stool across. 'I think you'd better sit down, Bat Maxwell.'

Maxwell sat and barked gruffly at a waitress for a whiskey. The two men sat in silence until the drink arrived, sizing each other up. Maxwell downed his drink in one swig and beckoned for another. 'You want one?' he asked Bogue.

Bogue nodded.

'I hear you're a feller who can find people,' Maxwell said.

'Maybe.'

'For a price, of course.'

'Depends on the person and depends on the price.'

'This feller doesn't want to be found,' Maxwell said.

'They rarely do. Who are we talking about? Anyone I might know?'

Maxwell drained the rest of his whiskey. 'Charlie Weston.'

Bogue lowered his glass slowly, trying to hide his surprise. 'Charlie Weston?' he asked, just to make sure he had heard correctly.

Maxwell nodded.

'Are you sure?'

Maxwell nodded again.

'It's going to cost you, that's all I'm going to say.'

'Do you know him?' Maxwell looked directly at Bogue.

'Know Charlie Weston? I know of him.'

'No,' Maxwell interrupted. 'I asked, do you know him?'

This time Bogue paused before replying and met Maxwell's glare dead on. At last, weighing his words carefully, he said, 'Yes, I know him.'

'Can you do it?' Maxwell said. 'I need to know if I'm wasting my time. I know you're both . . .'

'. . . outlaws,' Bogue finished the sentence for him.

'Yes.'

'That doesn't mean we're brothers,' Bogue said. 'How much are we talking about?'

Maxwell held his gaze. 'You're really willing to do this?'

Bogue nodded.

'Without even asking me why I want him killed?'

'You have the money, I'll pull the trigger.'

'Fine. Two thousand dollars.'

Bogue smiled.

'I've heard that you're the best,' Maxwell said, 'that's why I've made you such a generous offer. It's a lot of money, but if you want the best you have to pay for it, that's what I believe.'

'Up front.'

'No. Half now and half after. Or I find someone else.' From inside his coat Maxwell pulled out a leather satchel and passed it across the table.

Bogue opened it and looked inside.

The satchel was stuffed full of dollars. 'You won't find anyone as good as me.'

'You can count it, if you want,' Maxwell offered.

'No need.'

'My ranch is about five miles out of town. Anyone will tell you where it is, if you need me.'

Maxwell rose from the table and extended his hand toward Bogue. 'Good doing business with you.'

Bogue watched Maxwell's back as he walked toward the door, all the while keeping one hand on his gun and the other on the leather satchel of money.

He had one more drink after Maxwell left. The offer was a good one. Two thousand dollars was the most he'd ever been offered to kill a man. He could probably give up his gun if he succeeded in tracking down and killing Charlie Weston. But that was a big 'if'. Charlie Weston was a killer, just like him, and if Weston didn't want to be found, then things could get complicated.

Bogue left the saloon. His first

objective was to try and find some information that could help him track down Weston. With his insides warmed by the whiskey, he strolled along the boardwalk. He kept under the awnings of the buildings. Being a hired gunman meant he had his enemies and staying in the shadows was the safest course of action. It was impossible to tell when a relative of someone he'd killed would try and even up the score and restore some family pride.

He entered another saloon; a run-down, dingy establishment. Up on the raised stage two women danced, trying their best to attract the attention of customers who were steadily getting more and more drunk. A piano and a fiddle provided music and a feller swayed erratically around the floor, out of time with the tune. That feller was Chris McGraw.

Bogue grabbed McGraw by both shoulders and manoeuvred him toward a free table. A waitress came over but he waved her away. 'Hey, I want a whiskey!' McGraw whined as he tried to catch her skirt when she flounced off. 'In a minute,' Bogue barked. 'After you answer a few questions.'

McGraw's eyes were bloodshot and he smelled of stale sweat and smoke, yet, Bogue knew, this drunk was just the man he needed to talk to if he were to have any chance of collecting the second half of his bounty. McGraw spent his whole life drinking his way up and down the trails and knew every saloon and every man and woman that frequented them. He was regarded by all and sundry as a harmless drunkard; to be tolerated like a stray dog. But McGraw heard everything and remembered almost everything, despite his drinking. He was a long-time acquaintance of Bogue's and his pocket provided the money for a lot of McGraw's liquor. In return for a little information, of course.

'What you doing here, Bogue? This a social call or are you here to kill me?'

'Just some information,' Bogue replied.

'I don't want your blood money,'

McGraw spat. He got up to stand but fell to the floor, too drunk to walk.

Bogue picked him up and placed him back on his stool. 'I know,' Bogue said. 'But you need money and I need to hear what you know about Charlie Weston.'

McGraw cocked an eyebrow as best he could. 'Charlie Weston?' he slurred. 'You thinking of asking him to be your partner?' He smiled ruefully at his own joke. 'Or you just trying to take out your competition?'

'Something like that,' Bogue muttered. This time he called the waitress over. 'Two whiskies,' he told her and when they arrived he passed them both to McGraw, who drank them eagerly.

'You must want this guy badly,' McGraw said, his voice hoarse from the harsh burn of the whiskey. Bogue placed twenty dollars on the table. McGraw eyed them. Bogue still had his hand on them, both to make sure they weren't snatched and also to make sure that McGraw's drunken eyes couldn't miss them.

'All yours if you tell me what I want to know. We both know the routine and, to tell the truth, I don't have much time.'

'Fine,' McGraw said. 'Last I heard he was up in Baxter Springs. Bank job.'

'Same old Weston,' Bogue muttered.

'Nope,' McGraw replied, 'not this time. Something happened, I heard. Shortly after the bank job, he shows up in Lawrence and shoots up a couple of men.'

'Anything else?'

'Don't think so. Hadn't heard about him for a long time before that.'

Bogue nodded. He didn't know why Weston had suddenly resurfaced. Maybe he was broke? Maybe he liked the taste of stealing and shooting too much to give it up? It was in some people's blood. A fact he knew from personal experience. He rose to leave but stopped to ask one final question of McGraw. 'You know anything about Bat Maxwell?'

'Bat Maxwell? I know the name. He owns a lot of land around here. And cattle, too. His sons run most of it and he

64

just collects the money. I've met the sons, all right. Josiah and Dave. Didn't like them much, Josiah especially. Sneaky. You'd want to be careful if you're involved with Bat Maxwell. That much I do know. The only law he believes in is one that you carry in your holster. That's about it, I'm afraid.'

*Baxter Springs,* Bogue thought as he left the saloon. *I haven't been there in a long time.*

# 6

'I'd like to speak to the marshal,' the tall figure stated as he entered the jailhouse. His hat was pulled low, obscuring his face, which was just as well, as there was more than likely a bill with that face and a reward printed underneath it hanging somewhere in the building.

'Who's asking?' the man behind the table asked gruffly.

'A concerned citizen.'

Evan Taylor grunted at hearing this and chewed on his tobacco. He'd had enough of concerned citizens in the two weeks he'd been marshal to last him a lifetime. This job wasn't proving as enjoyable as he thought it would be. He'd imagined roaming around Baxter Springs, untouchable and unaccountable. The reality was somewhat different. The last thing he wanted that morning, as he nursed a heavy hangover from the night before, was someone coming into

66

his office asking awkward questions. But, he reasoned to himself, short of shooting this feller dead right there in front of him, at the very least he'd have to listen to what he had to say.

Taylor stood up slowly, giving his head a chance to catch up with his body, hoping that his queasiness eased a little. 'Well, citizen,' he asked, 'what're you so concerned about?'

'My name's Adam Crean,' the stranger said authoritatively as he offered his hand to Taylor. 'And I'm a Pinkerton.'

Taylor shook his hand roughly. 'A Pinkerton?' he asked, surprised. 'What business have you around here?'

'Powers Bank have employed me.'

'Oh,' Taylor muttered. 'You're here about the bank robbery. Well, I don't know nothing about that.'

This time it was Crean's turn to show surprise. 'What d'you mean, you don't know nothing about it? You're the marshal, aren't you?'

'Sure am.' Taylor paused as he spat out a wedge of chewing tobacco. 'But I wasn't when that happened.'

'But that was only two weeks ago. Did the last feller get shot or something? I hadn't heard.'

A smile crossed Taylor's face. 'A Pinkerton that don't know everything? Maybe you're not such a great detective after all?'

Crean's face reddened. 'My mistake,' he said. 'Maybe you'd tell me where I can find someone who does know about the robbery?'

Taylor still wore his stupid grin. 'Gee, I'm only a lawman two weeks and already I got a Pinkerton asking for my help,' he said.

Crean stared at Taylor. 'Afraid so, friend,' he said, forcing a smile. 'You've got the better of me here.'

Taylor chuckled deeply, savouring this small satisfaction. He could feel the pounding in his head returning, however, and decided that it was time to send this feller on his way.

'You're looking for Pete Baker,' he said. 'He was marshal when the bank was robbed, killed all the gang except the feller that had the money.' A flash of pain passed through his brain. His hangover was returning fast, and with a vengeance. 'You'll probably find him in the Ranchers' Saloon, his wife runs the place.'

'Much obliged,' the detective replied and tipped the brim of his hat. Taylor never did get a good look at Crean's face, as the Pinkerton turned and left him to his hangover.

* * *

Joe and Pete sat at the kitchen table in the back of the Ranchers' Saloon, listening to the sound of drunken customers that carried through from the bar.

'I thought we'd be able to leave this behind,' Pete said grimly. 'Bring Tom up out in the country on a homestead. This isn't a good place for a child.'

'I don't know,' Joe said. 'Dorothy grew up here and she turned out all right.'

Pete smiled. He could always rely on

Joe to stay positive, to say something to try and keep his spirits up. But he had had his heart set on a farming life, on leaving the Ranchers' Saloon behind. Now that dream seemed to be disappearing. The search for the outlaw wasn't going well and he'd come to realise that he'd acted rashly when he pledged to bring him in. In his role as marshal he had spent most of his time locking up drunken cowboys and trying to maintain as much peace as possible. Chasing all over the country-side following faint clues wasn't what he was used to. None of the dead robbers yielded any helpful information, either. They'd been outcasts, known up and down the trails as guns-for-hire; trouble-makers who'd do anything for the price of a drink.

Pete and Joe had quickly reached a dead end. The bitter truth was that there wasn't much appetite for helping the law in and around Baxter Springs, particularly when there was no reward on offer. And since it was known that Pete's days as a lawman were numbered it soon became obvious that his authority amongst the townsfolk had diminished, making his job that much more difficult, if not almost impossible.

'Maybe working in the saloon won't be so bad,' Pete mumbled. 'I'm sure I'd get used to it, eventually.'

'Sure,' Joe replied.

Pete slipped into a listless silence, absentmindedly listening to the singing and shouting from the saloon. There was nothing more to be said. Even Joe couldn't fill the void. They both drank their coffees.

'Pete,' Dorothy said as she entered the room, 'there's someone here to see you.'

A tall man with his hat low, obscuring his face, came in. He kept his long coat on as he sat in the chair Pete offered. All in all, Pete thought he was a strange-looking feller.

'Name's Pete Baker, and this here's Joe Flaherty. What can I do for you, stranger?'

'Adam Crean,' the man said. 'I'm here to ask you a few questions about the bank robbery.'

Pete and Joe looked at him, hard. 'What's your interest in the matter?' Pete asked.

'I'm a Pinkerton.'

'You employed by the bank?'

'Sure am.'

'Well then, let's all have some more coffee and then you can ask your questions.'

About an hour later, after much questioning and almost as much coffee, Adam Crean said he'd gotten all the information he sought and left the Ranchers' Saloon.

Pete waited until Crean left and then grabbed his hat from the back of the chair. 'Come on, Joe,' he said urgently.

Joe jumped to his feet, clearly surprised by this sudden call to action. 'Why?'

'We've got to follow him.'

'The Pinkerton?'

'That ain't no Pinkerton, Joe. That's Dan Bogue, and if he's interested in our robbery, then he might know something that could help us.'

They left the building as quickly as possible and from a safe distance followed Bogue down the street.

★ ★ ★

Bogue was preoccupied as he walked. He kept to the wooden boardwalk as much as possible, sticking to the shadows where he could. Baxter Springs was busy, the stores and saloons all doing brisk business. Horses snickered as they stood tied to hitching rails all along the street. He wasn't sure what to make of his meeting with Pete Baker. He'd learned all the details about the robbery, some of which McGraw had already provided. What Bogue discovered was that Weston had escaped somewhere on the plain and almost certainly killed one of his own men in the process. That wasn't good news. He knew that it meant Weston intended to disappear, maybe even retire, and hadn't planned on sharing the money. But then something had happened, some event had provoked his furious killing spree in the saloon in Lawrence, a piece of information the marshal didn't mention. Something that led to a price being put on Weston's head and drawn Dan Bogue into his story. A story that must end with Weston's death.

He'd come across Weston before but it was untrue to say that there was a sense of brotherhood or even empathy between the gunmen. They weren't soldiers. They weren't fighting for a greater cause. They were working for their own selfish needs. For material gain, and for power. And, no matter what concerns Bat Maxwell might have about Bogue's willingness to carry out his task, killing Charlie Weston carried no more significance for him than he might attach to squashing a bug underfoot. He slipped into a saloon; he needed a drink to help him think.

As always, he sat at a corner table to ensure that he held the whole saloon in his field of vision. He ordered a beer and when it arrived he took a thirsty mouthful.

He relaxed a little and began to run through the course of events involving Charlie Weston.

Weston had robbed a bank here in Baxter Springs and gotten away, but then turned up just down the road in Lawrence two weeks later, where he killed two men. There, the trail grew cold. As he considered what to do next, Bogue ordered a whiskey.

He felt the liquid easing his aching bones after the long ride to get there. He sat, taking stock, debating what to do next.

★ ★ ★

Pete watched Bogue emerge from the saloon; he had only been a few minutes. Evening was creeping in and twilight descending on the town. Bogue turned left and made his way along the busy street. Pete set off after him at a brisk pace, Joe just behind.

Bogue walked determinedly, rarely breaking his stride. He kept to the sides of

75

the street and occasionally looked from left to right, surveying the passers-by.

Pete stayed well back, trying to remain as inconspicuous as possible. Bogue took a sharp turn to his right, leaving the street abruptly. He entered the Hakluyt Hotel. Pete paused, unsure what to do now. Follow him inside or stay? He lingered outside the hotel. He couldn't see anything but the dull interior of the entrance hallway. He stepped in off the street.

Bogue was nowhere to be seen.

Pete immediately crossed the lobby.

'What can I do for you?' asked the man behind the reception desk. He paused before adding, 'Marshal.'

'I need a little help, Benjamin,' Pete said as Joe now joined him.

'Anything you ask, Pete.'

Benjamin Hakluyt had been running his hotel since before Pete came to town, and Pete had had few dealings with him. Any time they met, Hakluyt seemed polite and courteous. He valued peace and quiet, but he also valued his guests' privacy, Pete knew. That meant that he had always complied with Pete, but he was aware of where the law ended and his rights began. This could be difficult, Pete mused. But he needed Benjamin's help and he was going to have to get it, one way or another.

'That man who just came in. Is he a guest of yours?'

Benjamin paused before answering, obviously thinking over the implications of anything he would say. 'Yes, he is. Why do you ask, Pete? Last I heard, you weren't doing any more law work around the town. Heard you were trying to catch the *bandidos* that robbed the bank.'

'That's right.' Pete took a deep breath before continuing. 'It's like this, Ben. That feller who just walked up your stairs is a murderer. A gun for hire. His picture's hanging in the jailhouse.'

The colour drained from the hotelier's face.

'Now, either you're going to keep an eye on him for me, and tell me personally when he's leaving or I'm going to tell

Evan Taylor that Dan Bogue's hiding out in your hotel. And I can only imagine the kind of damage Evan would do to these fine premises of yours if he should come in here to arrest this man.'

Ben nodded and then spoke very softly: 'Yes, Marshal.'

'So, I want to know if he looks like he's going to leave town. Is that clear?' He didn't wait for a reply. 'You're a good man, Benjamin; I know you'll do the right thing.'

He gestured to Joe and they left the premises and returned to the street, leaving a troubled Ben Hakluyt behind.

'Gee, Pete. Weren't you a bit harsh with him?' Joe asked.

'I didn't enjoy that. He's a good man; too good. He'd think the best of all his customers and wouldn't tell us a thing without some persuasion. Evan Taylor certainly helped us out there, even if he don't know it.'

'It's the only way he'd ever help us,' Joe replied, laughing.

They headed down the street, back

toward the Ranchers' Saloon, with a spring in their step. Progress, at last, Pete thought. He wasn't sure what kind of progress, but at least things were moving forward.

\* \* \*

As the two lawmen walked past an alleyway, they didn't take any notice of the cowboy lighting a match off the sole of his boot. But the cowboy noticed them; he'd been waiting for them, and kept a safe distance from them until they had entered the saloon.

Confident that they were more than likely in there for the night, he returned to the alleyway near the Hakluyt Hotel and watched the doorway, waiting for any sign of Dan Bogue.

\* \* \*

Joe and Pete sat heavily at the kitchen table once more. Dorothy was with them, holding baby Tom in her arms.

Pete gestured to her and she passed the baby across and watched as her husband stared lovingly into the eyes of his son. Something was amiss, she could tell. Pete wasn't much of a one for deception and he could never keep his true feelings from her. She held her tongue, however, and allowed father and son time together. He'd tell her when the time was right.

She bustled about and poured coffee for herself and the two men. They looked weary, she thought. Inwardly, she'd reconciled herself to the fact that Pete would lose his job when the two months were up. He didn't seem to have made any inroads into the solving of the case, despite an enthusiastic start, and both he and Joe now seemed to spend their whole time sitting at her kitchen table, drinking coffee and staring into space.

But something was different today. A light had returned to Pete's eyes. Something had happened. She couldn't hold back any longer, it wasn't in her nature. She was a woman who called a spade a spade and said things as they were. Time to get everything out in the open. Pete often thought that he was protecting her, she knew, by sparing her the details of his work but she always got them out of him. And, she was sure, he was always glad she did.

'Spit it out, you two,' she whispered, trying not to wake the now sleeping baby. 'Something's after happening and I won't be left out.'

Pete looked up at her with a wry smile, while Joe just concentrated on his coffee.

'I was just about to tell you, darling,' he said. His voice was lighter, as if some of the lethargy that smothered him in the previous weeks had dissipated.

'Well then, get on with the telling.'

Pete explained to her about Dan Bogue, a hired gun, not a Pinkerton detective, and told her of their conversation with Benjamin Hakluyt.

'I hope you didn't scare Ben too bad,' she scolded. 'I hear Jane talking about his heart all the time.'

'He knows the right thing to do. That's all that matters.'

'Well, what are you fixing to do?' She couldn't keep the worry from her voice. On the one hand, she was happy to see her husband regaining his sense of purpose, while on the other, she was worried where it might lead him. She could already feel that it might take him away from her for a time; she could only pray that it would allow him to return.

Pete took a deep breath. He looked down on the sleeping figure of Tom, all swaddled up in his blanket, just his soft face uncovered. Dorothy beckoned for him to pass the baby over but he shook his head and held his son even closer, feeling the warmth of his body. Everything was here in Baxter Springs: Dorothy, Tom, even Cal, his father-in-law, and of course Joe, his friend. All the family he had in the world. Was he foolish, was he being stupid or rash or reckless in what he planned to do?

Then he thought about the man Dorothy married. Thought of what life had been like when he'd been marshal, doing something he loved until the politics of the position interfered. In truth, the last few weeks were a blur of depression, indolence and dissatisfaction. He hadn't been himself, something he hadn't even really realized or acknowledged until Dan Bogue walked into their kitchen and energised him like a bolt of lightning. He must continue; he had to see it through. It wasn't just for him, it was for all of them. If he was successful, he was sure he could make a better life for his family. He must find the bank robber.

'When Bogue leaves town, Joe and I will be going after him,' Pete said eventually. His voice was steady as he desperately fought back the emotions that welled inside. 'He knows something about the robbery and I intend finding out what it is. He might lead us right to the culprit.'

'Or he might kill you,' Dorothy said quickly.

'I'll be careful. You know that. I can look after myself.'

'I know,' she said softly. 'I know.' Tears brimmed in her eyes and slid slowly down her cheeks.

Joe pushed his chair back from the table. 'I better go home and get my things. I might not have time later.' He left, hurriedly.

After they placed Tom in his crib, Dorothy and Pete headed for their bedroom. When they got there, Dorothy clasped her arms around Pete and kissed him hard on the lips. 'I'm sure Dan Bogue won't leave town tonight,' she whispered softly.

The knock on the door came early the next morning. Joe and Pete were ready and waiting.

'He's checking out,' Benjamin's son, Amos, said breathlessly.

Pete kissed baby Tom and Dorothy goodbye, his hand lingering on her shoulder as he pulled her to him. 'See you soon,' he said.

Dorothy couldn't muster any words as he left. Tears ran down her face, obscuring what she feared was her last sight of her husband.

# 7

Weston quickly came to learn that life on the trail was a hard routine. At first light, the shouts of the sentries drew the bleary-eyed men and women from their tents and wagons. Then the day's routine started: rounding up the cows that had been left to graze on the nearby meadow and bringing them in ready for the trek; collecting buffalo chips and starting fires; cooking breakfasts, stowing away blankets, striking camp, yoking oxen.

Once under way, the men walked beside their teams, giving an occasional flick of the whip over their animals, while the women and children often broke off from the column to pick wild flowers. Around noon, there'd be a break, preferably by a stream, when a light meal was taken — very quickly, so that it wasn't worth unyoking the oxen. Already, Weston saw the travellers growing weary.

The afternoon was a sleepy time.

Women and children usually took the opportunity for a nap in the wagons while drivers seemed to nod off as they walked. Even the oxen appeared to doze as they plodded along. As night came they circled their wagons to protect against possible Indian attacks. Outside the wagons, they pitched their tents, and then in the outer perimeter, they built their fires. Within the inner corral of wagons, they kept the precious horses and mules.

Since there was no room for the cattle inside the corral, and as Indians were reputed not to be too interested in stealing them, they were turned loose on the plain; the emigrants hoped that, come morning, they wouldn't have been stampeded by lightning storms or spooked by a buffalo herd. Meanwhile, children collected buffalo chips for the fire while the women prepared the evening meal — typically salt meat, fresh-baked bread and black coffee.

The period after dinner was the best part of the day. This was the time when men spun yarns with gusto around the campfires and decisions were made at a full meeting. This was the type of society that Charlie Weston had now joined.

On the day after the meeting, Chet had returned the Colt to Weston. Betty seemed glad that he had stayed. If nothing else, he was someone else for her to talk to, talking being her favourite pastime. Weston humoured her. He plied her with questions about the others in the group and she was more than ready to supply answers. He learned that the four wagons were indeed filled with four different families.

Besides Chet and Betty, there were Frank Giles and his wife Kit. Travelling with them was their sixteen-year-old son, Will. He resembled his father and seemed to carry his antipathy toward Weston, too, judging by the malevolent glares he shot in his direction. Will usually spent his time riding along the train on his saddle horse, showing off for Emmet McCann's daughter.

Another wagon was driven by Walt

Butters with his wife, Maria. They had a six-year-old son named Mark and a daughter, Anna, who was four.

Leading the small train was Emmet McCann's wagon. Emmet sat up front with his wife Angie, while his twenty-three-year-old daughter, Rose, rode alongside on her horse. She was a fine specimen, Weston thought, if a little young for him. She was a full fifteen years his junior, but with her curly blonde hair and full figure, she sure was easy on the eye.

Will Giles seemed to be constantly by her side but, Weston thought, his attentions didn't seem altogether well received.

He certainly wasn't going to get involved, even if he didn't like the cocky swagger Will affected.

Each day, Weston relaxed a little more; the more ground he put between him and Lawrence the better. Even though their pace was slow, he was pretty sure that Maxwell's men would never think to look for him in an emigrant train. Of course, if they were to track him down. . . ? That didn't bear thinking about. The more time he spent in Chet and Betty's company, the more he got to like them. He knew he was putting them in danger but he didn't think he had any other choice. California, or Fort Laramie at least, seemed as good a place as any to hide from Maxwell.

'So, Chet,' Weston said over supper, 'what inspired you to leave home and head west? Gold, I'll wager.' A flicker of a smile crossed Weston's face at his jest.

Chet went quiet for a moment before he answered. 'That's a real tough question,' he replied. 'I'm not sure if there's any one answer.' He looked at Betty and she nodded in agreement. 'I suppose I've always been a kind of restless feller. Left home when I was young to go fight in Mexico. Wanted to see different places. My parents weren't happy with me, mind, but they did welcome me back when I returned. Bad memories and all. I fought the Union, too,' he added wistfully. 'War is a bad thing, Weston, of that there can be no doubt. There's nothing noble about it, and I should know at this stage. At the end of the day, all you've got is a load of fellers either screaming in pain or dying in a ditch.'

He went silent; Weston could see that he was dredging up some painful memories.

'When I came home I worked the family farm. Married Betty, the girl next door, the best thing I ever did.' He clasped her hand affectionately. 'But when my folks died, I realized that there was nothing else holding us there. We have no children and I suppose the travelling bug bit me again. Life is short, war taught me that at least, and I plan on packing as much as I can into what I've got left of mine. Part of that plan is this journey. We'll see what happens when we get to California. I just hope you weren't lying when you said that you can help us get to where we're going. We'll be at the Platte soon enough. I sure hope we all make it to the other side.' He rose and headed back to the wagon with Betty, his candour leaving Weston silent.

Weston had never met such conviction in anyone before. Such quiet determination, drive and focus. He'd thought of Chet as some easygoing feller who took life as it came, someone he thought himself superior to and could maybe manipulate if necessary. He'd been mistaken, he now realised. His quiet purposefulness sparked something inside Charlie Weston, something he couldn't quite define. It made him look at his situation anew.

The next few days, Weston kept to himself, digesting what Chet had said. He hadn't really thought about what he could do to help the wagoners, just what he could get from them. Namely food, shelter and escape. All his pronouncements about being able to help them reach their destination had been insincere; he'd merely been trying to save his own skin. But now, as the broad, muddy Platte loomed into view, he knew that he could and would help them, at least for the time being. He owed Chet that much, at least.

The wagons drew to a halt along the river's low bank. It must have been a mile across at that point, shallow, but rapid-running.

'The Platte,' Weston said to no one in particular.

'You don't say,' Will Giles replied smartly. The only person who laughed was his father; Rose didn't even look at him. Seeming eager to get her attention he said in his high-pitched voice, 'I hear that the bottom is pure quicksand.' This time a look of fear crossed Rose's face. However, it was Weston she turned to for reassurance, not Will. In fact, by now all the emigrants turned to Weston, even Emmet McCann.

'It's not quicksand,' Weston said with firm authority. 'The bottom is sand, all right, but smooth and well packed. We'll make it across.'

'Why should we believe you?' Frank Giles demanded. 'How do we know that you don't want to drown us all in this river and take all our belongings?'

'I guess you don't know that,' Weston

replied drolly.

'What's that supposed to mean?' Frank asked aggressively. He stalked over toward Weston.

Weston faced him and clenched his fists, ready to lash out.

Giles stopped inches from him, their faces almost touching. 'I never wanted you to come with us!' Frank roared. 'You're trouble and you're not going to kill me and my family crossing that river.'

Will Giles had ridden over and his horse now snorted and stamped near Weston, urged on by its rider.

Weston ignored Will and focused completely on Frank. He stared hard into his eyes, his steely gaze causing Frank to flinch just a little. 'I don't care what you or your son think of me,' he said quietly and evenly, the menace in his voice only amplified by the controlled manner in which he spoke. 'I don't owe you anything. The only people who matter to me here are Chet and Betty.'

He felt surprised with himself even as he said these words. He hadn't planned what he was going to say, but the words just sounded right. They came naturally. 'Chet saved my life and I intend to get him as far as Fort Laramie, at the least. We'll be crossing that river,' he stabbed a hand toward the Platte, 'and you can come if you want. I really don't care.'

He turned his back to Giles and made his way over to Chet's wagon.

'Let's go, Chet,' he muttered.

He directed him to move on along the southern shore of the river.

Late that evening, they came to what Weston knew was a relatively shallow part of the river and he called the wagons to a halt. 'We'll camp here,' he said. 'We'll ford tomorrow.' His tone was stern and brooked no argument. They were all tired after a long day's travelling and quickly settled the animals and ate their supper. Weston went to sleep early; he would need all his energy for tomorrow.

# 8

Sleep didn't come easily to Weston. The fording of the river dominated his thoughts. He could hear it from where he lay, sweeping inexorably along on its way to the sea. He had told the truth when he said that he'd forded it before, but that was on horseback with nobody to worry about but himself. It would be a different matter with boxy, bulky, unwieldy wagons laden with people and belongings.

He thought of the children. Up to this point, he hadn't interacted much with them, or they with him. They seemed a little scared of him. But he didn't want to see them being washed to their deaths, either. The best thing he could do tonight was to try and get some sleep and be as alert as possible tomorrow. He reached into his coat pocket once more. Still there.

Was all this worth it? That was a question he'd never asked himself before.

About anything he'd done. He always acted on instinct, like some kind of animal. If he wanted something, he took it. Things had changed since he met Chet and the others, though. Maybe there was more to life? Maybe he could think of somebody else other than himself for a change? Tired from all this internal philosophising, he drifted off into a dreamless sleep.

\* \* \*

Emmet McCann was just about to drop off to sleep, too, when he felt a hand on his shoulder.

'Frank,' he exclaimed as he looked up into Giles' face, 'you scared me half to death.'

'Sorry, Emmet, but I've got to talk to you.'

'Can't it wait until morning?' McCann asked, knowing full well that it couldn't.

'No, Emmet.'

McCann sighed wearily.

'You're supposed to be in charge,

here,' Giles hissed, 'and you let this feller do what he likes. You let him tell us what to do!'

Emmet knew that what Frank said was true. He wasn't too happy with Weston either but couldn't see many other options open to him. Emmet had never crossed the Platte, and he explained this to Giles. It would be foolish not to take help when it was offered, he reasoned. Giles was exasperated.

'I think you're lily-livered, McCann. You're not fit to lead us. And if you're not careful, I might just do something about it.'

His words hung menacingly in the air, firing McCann's temper.

'Now you listen here! You'll do as I tell you,' McCann's voice shook with temper. He was tired from the day's travelling, groggy from want of sleep and aggravated by Giles' constant niggling. His tolerance had reached its end. 'He said he'll get us across the Platte and I believe he will. I've got to.'

He could see that Giles was about to

speak again so he cut him off with a wave of his hand. 'We'll see how things are once we get to Fort Laramie.' Weariness engulfed him, his sudden surge of temper having passed. 'I've nothing more to say to you, Frank.'

Giles rose and headed away without another word, but mumbled to himself: 'We'll see who makes it across the river.'

* * *

Weston woke first the next morning and made his way to the riverbank. The river seemed to be flowing faster than yesterday, and the distance to be covered seemed even greater. 'Just my imagination,' he muttered, more in hope than belief. Soon, he had mustered the men, even the two Gileses, and they dug a cutting into the bank in order to make a pathway to run the wagons down to the water. It was hard, physical work but they made steady progress and finished in the late morning, the activity giving the men something to concentrate their energies on.

* * *

'What next?' Chet asked Weston when the cutting was complete.

'The horses,' he replied.

'Water seems to be moving real fast.'

All the men had gathered around him now, eager to learn what was to happen next. They looked at him doubtfully. Weston could sense their worry. While they'd been digging, their minds were occupied, but now that they'd stopped, they could dwell on the task before them. Weston sensed their worry. 'It's shallow,' he replied.

'Maybe there's another fording point?' McCann asked. 'Maybe there's a ferry or a bridge?'

This suggestion drew a murmur of agreement from all present, including the women who had come over to listen to the discussion.

Weston stalked away from them and grabbed one of the saddle horses, frustration at their reluctance to trust him flaring within him.

'Hey,' Will Giles called, 'that's my horse.'

Weston ignored him and pulled himself up into the saddle. He spurred the horse forward. The men had to move fast to get out of his way as he rode past them and down the cutting into the cold water of the Platte. As man and horse fought against the power of the current the animal's head dipped and water splashed up around its neck. For a moment, Weston was worried as the frightened horse struggled to find its footing on the riverbed.

'Easy,' he soothed. 'Easy, boy.'

The horse was strong and it battled hard to regain its balance. Weston sat back in the saddle and gradually the animal pulled its head and front legs up. It had found some purchase on the riverbed. Weston felt the power of the animal returning and he urged him on across the current. Now that it had confidence in its footing, the horse pressed on and made for land as fast as possible, crossing the river in as straight a line as it could, the water barely reaching half way up its flank.

Weston held on tight to the reins and squeezed the horse's flanks with his thighs to help keep his balance. They struggled on, battling across the current for what seemed like an eternity until, at last, they found the opposite bank. He urged his mount on once more and the horse pulled itself out of the river without much effort, water dripping from its flanks.

Safe on the northern shore, Weston turned to face the southern bank. There was barely a reaction from the others but then someone let out a cheer that reverberated across the river and this was the signal for the rest to join in. Weston, not knowing what possessed him, thrust his arm in the air in triumph, drawing even louder shouts of acclaim. He'd done it.

Now he just had to get the rest of the wagoners across.

★ ★ ★

McCann called everyone together the next morning.

'Thanks for yesterday, Charlie. We owe you a lot,' he said.

A murmur of agreement spread through the group.

McCann knew that the Giles men wouldn't be happy with his praise of Weston but he felt that it was something he had to do. Even a blind man could see that without him the crossing could have been disastrous.

Yet Giles had made a valid point in their earlier conversation. He, Emmet McCann, was in charge, not Charlie Weston, and he still believed that he was the best man to keep the group together and get them safely to California. It was time to reassert his authority.

'Next town is Fort Laramie, some four hundred miles away. A lot of the journey is over open country and there may be some Indians. This ain't going to be easy. Remember, I'm in charge, so if I give an order, we all abide by it. It might be the difference between life and death out there.'

'That's for sure,' Weston muttered to himself. There was plenty of death where they were headed.

\* \* \*

Travelling was peaceful for the next few days with no sign of any danger. Weston felt a serenity that he had not experienced for a long time. This escape from society, living in this small, enclosed community seemed to suit him. But he knew that it couldn't last forever, just as he knew that he couldn't stick it forever, either. He was a wanted man, the pouch in his inside pocket reminded him of that, but he pushed these thoughts to the back of his mind. He wanted to see where this particular journey would take him.

He stared vacantly ahead, immersed in his thoughts, seeing but not really seeing, until something pierced his daydreaming and brought him back to reality.

A figure on horseback pulled alongside him.

'Do I look funny or something?' asked the rider, Rose.

Weston was caught by surprise.

'N–no,' he stammered. 'Why do you ask?'

'No reason.' She paused for a moment and then added, 'Just that you've been staring at me for the last ten minutes.'

Weston felt the blood rush to his cheeks. 'I'm sorry,' he said quickly. 'I was daydreaming. I didn't even know where I was looking. I could have been staring at a cow, for all I knew.'

The hurt on Rose's face told him immediately that he had said exactly the wrong thing.

'I mean . . .'

'Forget it,' she said defiantly and sharply pulled her horse away.

Weston watched her ride off and shook his head as she pulled alongside Will Giles. He stared at her back, angry with himself and his stupidity, yet not really understanding why. True, she was beautiful, but why did he care? His thoughts of Rose were immediately pushed to the back of his mind by a call from Butters' son, Mark: 'Buffalo!' he bellowed.

The young boy pointed into the middle distance toward a great mass of brown hide. His feelings of wonder and excitement were obvious in his voice. A herd of buffalo grazed about a mile away, just beyond a small watercourse. They looked so sturdy and their coats so brown that Chet Harrington was prompted to comment that they looked like a small forest. The train came to a halt as they studied the grazing animals. The men dismounted and grouped together.

'This is what I came to see,' Chet mumbled.

'What d'you mean?' Frank Giles asked gruffly.

'I mean,' Chet replied patiently, 'that we would never have seen this at home. This journey is as important to Betty and me as the destination.'

'This is ridiculous,' Giles snorted. 'I'm here for one reason only, to make money. We're heading to a land of plenty and the sooner we get there the better.

That's the reason I'm here.'

Chet was quiet. There was no reply to that. He had always found Frank Giles difficult and now he knew for definite that they had absolutely nothing in common. They would never see eye to eye but he wasn't going to let it get to him. That was life and it took all kinds. Just like Weston. He looked across at the man who was still a relative stranger to him even though he'd been with them for the past week. All in his own good time, he mused. Weston would reveal himself. The prairie forces that from a man, he reckoned.

'I don't know about you,' Emmet McCann proclaimed, 'but I think this is a great chance to get us some meat.'

Giles nodded. 'Let me get my rifle.'

'Me too,' Walt Butters added.

'You going?' Chet asked Weston.

'Well, I'm not so sure . . .' Then Weston grinned. 'Yeah, I'd like to eat some fresh meat as opposed to the tough salted stuff we've had the last few days — no offence.'

'None taken. I feel the same.'

'Then let's go, Chet,' Weston said. 'Otherwise those fellers will only scare away the buffalo.'

Weston rode off, quickly overtaking McCann, Butters and Giles. He had little faith in the hunting ability of the others. He felt that he needed to lead the way, not follow.

He couldn't help but notice the look of malevolence that crossed Giles' face as he rode past him, however.

They rode to a creek that stood between them and the herd of buffalo.

Weston dismounted and tied his horse to a fallen tree.

Giles was next to arrive and followed suit and when McCann and Butters got there, they'd already gone ahead.

Weston heard twigs breaking underfoot behind him and he hissed at his follower to be quiet. He didn't look to see who it was but soon found out as Giles' fist crashed into the side of his head, sending him tumbling to the ground. His ears rang and a shuddering numbness spread through his head.

Before he knew what was happening, Giles was upon him, fists swinging again.

Weston raised his hands up to protect himself, absorbing the blows on his arms as best he could.

Giles grunted as he expended his energy on Weston's upper body until strong arms gripped him from behind and he found himself lifted bodily from the ground.

'What d'you think you're doing?' McCann barked, tightening his grip on Giles' midriff.

'What you should've done a long time ago,' he shouted, flecks of spittle flying from his mouth. 'Straightened this crook out. He'll kill us.'

'I'm in charge,' McCann said, 'and if anyone needs straightening out, it's you!'

'You're a fool.'

McCann let go of the struggling Giles.

Weston slowly regained his feet and dusted himself down. He ached a little and his head felt a bit woolly but he wasn't seriously hurt. He walked over toward the others.

'You OK?' Butters asked as he drew close.

Weston heard him but just brushed by. His fist flashed out so fast that Giles didn't even see it coming. It connected flush with his chin and Giles was out cold before he even hit the ground.

'Let's hunt some buffalo,' Weston said gruffly.

Butters and McCann stared at the prone figure on the ground.

'He really ain't going to be happy, now,' Butters said wryly. McCann just nodded.

Weston was glad to see that the buffalo hadn't been startled away by his altercation with Giles. He made a mental note to pay more attention to that hothead. He'd been caught by surprise, something that hurt Weston more than the blows that had rained down on him. He was slipping, that was the moral of the story. He'd have to sharpen up. All this peaceful trekking around the prairie must be making him soft.

The three men stopped behind a fallen tree about a hundred yards from the herd. Weston raised his rifle and aimed at the nearest buffalo. Butters and McCann did the same.

The air was filled first with the sound of their shots and then the pounding of hoofs. Dust kicked up by the escaping animals obscured Weston's view.

Eventually, the dust settled and they got a clear view. No buffalo remained on the plain; they'd disappeared over the small hill.

'Missed,' Butters mumbled disconsolately.

Weston cursed under his breath. He knew from experience that it took a lot to bring a buffalo down.

They got to their feet and turned and began to walk away when he heard the sound of hoofs behind them.

A lone buffalo appeared on the cusp of the hill and meandered slowly toward the watering hole, oblivious to the reason the rest of his companions had scattered so suddenly.

Weston watched intently as the animal approached their position, apparently ignorant of their presence. Weston raised his rifle. The animal drew closer, puffing and grunting as he plodded along the hard prairie ground. He was within range now and Weston pressed the stock of his rifle against his shoulder. As the animal reached the bottom of the bank and lowered his head to drink Weston's muscles tensed as he prepared to pull the trigger.

Butters wasn't as composed as Weston, however. His finger twitched as he steadied his gun, pulling the trigger and firing wildly toward the buffalo. The report from his weapon was rapidly followed by those of McCann's and Weston's. Weston knew immediately that they had missed, Butters' shot having startled the animal.

It seemed as if the world stood still for a moment. Weston's ears rang with the noise of the guns. The buffalo was still standing but with his head raised, staring directly toward them. He'd been nicked; blood welled on his flank. Not enough to kill him but just enough to make him angry.

The buffalo crouched, lowered his head and started pawing the ground. He was ready to fight.

Weston quickly lowered his rifle and turned to the two others. 'We're in trouble,' he said.

The expression on McCann's and Butters' faces showed that they thought the same.

The buffalo emitted a wild roar, a primal bellow.

Weston frantically searched for somewhere they could escape to. He didn't trust his rifle to stop the animal in time; it certainly hadn't worked thus far.

'The cottonwood,' he cried urgently, pointing to a tree just along the creek. It grew at an angle, curving gently up from the ground.

Butters began to speak but another roar from the buffalo quickly quieted him. 'Go!' Weston cried.

The three men ran toward the tree.

Weston led the way and scrambled furiously up its trunk. Butters followed closely behind and the two men quickly gained the cover and support of the few branches that grew on the tree.

McCann was having difficulty finding purchase on the bark with his boots, however. He struggled manfully but he could make no progress, his feet slipping.

The buffalo ran, his deep and powerful bellowing growing louder with each passing moment. McCann looked up at Weston and Butters, safely ensconced above him. There was terror in his eyes, Weston saw. He was angry with himself. The hunt, the feel of the rifle, the attempt to kill had brought back sensations that he thought he had buried. He was consumed by the drive to survive at the expense of all others. That was what he was used to; it had been his way of life for so long that he knew he'd been foolish to believe that it was a flame that could be quenched so easily.

*Look after yourself, first and only*, had long been his motto and way of life. That was why he worked alone, didn't form any attachments. Any lasting ones, at least. He cursed loudly, berating himself for staying with the company. For not stealing a horse the first night and riding away as he should have done. He'd grown soft, that was why he was hiding up a tree from a charging buffalo. And that was also why he knew he had to get Emmet McCann into the same position.

He thrust his rifle into Butters' hands and slid down the tree trunk, landing lightly on the hard ground.

'What?' McCann began but Weston silenced him.

The buffalo was only yards away now, the ground vibrating with the pounding of his hoofs as he charged.

'Give me your foot,' Weston barked.

McCann placed his right boot onto Weston's cupped hands.

'Go!'

McCann put all his weight onto the platform Weston made with his hands and propelled himself up the trunk. He still wasn't up high enough, however, but he held on for dear life to the tree trunk, just five feet above the ground. Weston put his shoulder under McCann's boot.

'Climb!' he shouted.

McCann pushed down with his feet once more and gained a little more height so that Butters could reach down with his free hand and pull him to safety.

Weston felt the weight lift from off his shoulders and looked up to see McCann safely beside Butters. Now all he had to worry about was the mass of angry buffalo hide hurtling toward him.

He allowed himself one quick look over his shoulder. His vision was filled by the shaggy outline of the animal. Instinctively, his reflexes acting almost before the command entered his mind, he surged upwards. His hands gripped the bark but he felt them slipping. He kicked at the trunk frantically, his boots beating out a rapid tattoo across the prairie.

After what seemed like an age but

was only a few seconds, he found a foothold and moved up the tree. And not a moment too soon.

The cottonwood vibrated as the buffalo butted it hard with his head, less than a foot below where Weston hung.

No matter, he was safe now. He looked up and took McCann's hand, the man helping him the rest of the way. Weston accepted gratefully.

The three men sat forlornly on the branches of the cottonwood as the buffalo raged and stamped about its base.

'What do we do now?' Butters asked, unable to hide the tremor in his voice.

Weston reached across and retrieved his rifle. The way Butters looked, he didn't trust him not to drop it.

'We get some buffalo steaks,' Weston replied grimly. 'No point in going through all this for nothing.'

He raised his rife and fired rapidly yet calmly into the vast body of the buffalo below. After a moment's pause, Butters and McCann fired their weapons too. At last the animal emitted a weary roar, a death yell, and keeled over. His legs ceased to kick and the creek nearby ran red with his blood.

That night the men were greeted with great joy as they rode back into camp with their two bags full of buffalo meat.

Weston ate alone and left the telling of the story of how the buffalo was killed to McCann and Butters. He felt the cold, angry glare of Frank Giles boring into his back as he ate.

*Things are getting complicated*, Weston mused, as he stared at Rose's soft features, lit up by the light of the campfire.

# 9

Their bellies were still full from their feed of steaks as they broke camp the next morning. As they travelled, ahead of them appeared a vertical column of sandstone in the distance, some forty feet high. A rugged stone bluff rose abruptly in front of it.

'That must be Chimney Rock,' Chet said excitedly. This was a famous landmark of the trail.

All eyes were drawn to this natural feature except Weston's. He gazed into the middle distance at something none of the others had seen. 'Sioux,' he muttered.

A low cloud of dust heralded the approach of the Indians.

Weston looked around the train. As usual, Rose was on her horse, well away from her parents' wagon. She had drifted behind, along with young Giles, something that she was prone to doing.

Weston didn't know whether she willingly spent time with Giles or not but right now he didn't care. One thing he knew for sure, though, was that Giles wouldn't be much use if the Sioux took a liking to Rose, and that was something that could happen very easily.

He shouted and waved toward Rose and Giles but they didn't seem to hear him.

There mightn't be any trouble, Weston reasoned. In fact, there usually wasn't. Often the Indians just wanted to trade. Weston felt uneasy about this group, however. As they neared, he noticed there were a lot of young braves among the twenty or so riders. *This could lead to complications*, he thought. Younger braves could be more aggressive, full of bravado and eager to show off, he knew from experience. Without the presence of the chief or an elder, they might prove difficult, especially if anything went wrong. *And, with a feller like Frank Giles in the train, this was a distinct possibility*, Weston thought.

'Emmet,' Weston called as he pointed toward the Sioux. He saw the worry that crossed the older man's face, quickly followed by panic as he cast about for his daughter.

'I'll get her,' Weston said.

'No, she's my daughter. I should do it.'

'I have something I need you to do,' Weston replied. They hadn't much time, he knew. He needed to relay his instructions quickly. 'I need you to ride to the Indian camp and talk to their chief. You're our commander. He'll listen to what you have to say. That should help make sure that there isn't any trouble because, to tell the truth, I don't like the look of these braves. Offer to trade with the chief. That should keep them happy.' He pointed to the vague outline of tents in the distance.

McCann knew he was right. He mounted up and, with Chet Harrington by his side, rode hard, straight past the approaching Sioux.

Weston hefted himself up onto the

back of the nearest horse and set off at full gallop toward Rose. He closed the gap quickly until, eventually, Rose and Will noticed him approaching.

'It's Weston,' Rose said.

'What's he waving about for?' Giles asked. 'That man's a fool anyhow, nearly got Emmet and Walt killed hunting that buffalo. I don't know why everyone was so proud of him.'

'There must be something wrong,' Rose replied. 'Come on.'

She urged her horse onward, toward Weston.

She saw the band of Sioux approaching the wagons, and worryingly, four of the horsemen had branched off and were heading straight for her. She dug her heels in again but she knew it would do no good. It was too late.

The Indians cut across her path, separating her from Weston. She tried to change direction but it was pointless. Where could she go? She had the wagon train and that was it. There was nothing more for her out there. Will rode up beside her.

'I told you we should have stayed closer to the wagons,' he said angrily. He was terrified; she could hear it in his voice.

'Bit late for that, now, don't you think?' Rose had marginally more success in hiding her fear. The four riders drew abreast of them, so close that Rose could see the sunlight reflected in their eyes.

'Just keep moving,' Rose muttered to Giles. 'Keep heading for the wagons, they might leave us alone.'

★ ★ ★

Butters cocked his rifle. Frank Giles had just ridden off after Weston toward his son, meaning that he was the only man left now and he had four women and two children to look after.

The band of Sioux drew up in front of him and one brave dismounted. Butters counted sixteen of them. All lean and strong. All young. All unpredictable.

Butters kept his rifle by his side, ready to use at any moment.

The Indian said something that Butters didn't understand but he took it as a welcome and muttered back: 'Howdy yourself.'

The young brave was a fine specimen of physical manhood, as were his companions. He was tall and well proportioned and carried himself with an air of great importance and dignity. He wore buckskin breeches and moccasins and a five-point Mackinaw blanket draped over his shoulders. Butters had never come face to face with an Indian before and he wished he had someone else beside him to help him out. Preferably Weston. Sweat rolled down his forehead. He used the back of his hand to wipe it before it dripped into his eyes. He swallowed; his throat was parched.

Running through his head were all the stories he'd heard about the savagery of the Sioux, of scalpings, in particular. He'd also heard that those days were in the past, at least in these parts, and he sincerely hoped that was the case. He glanced behind him to ensure his family were safe. His wife had her arms around their young children. They didn't seem to know whether they should be frightened or excited. Their eyes were as round as bowls as they watched the mounted men stalk around their wagons.

'Biscuit?' the brave suddenly asked Butters.

Butters called to his wife, 'Get him some biscuit, quick!'

Betty Harrington and Angie McCann dashed to their wagons and when all had returned, the brave had a fine haul of biscuits handed to him. He turned and smiled to his companions and it seemed to Butters that the whole band grinned back.

'Tobac!'

This time it was more of a demand than a request but Butters didn't think he was in a position to refuse. He heard the women scurrying about between the wagons, getting some tobacco together.

Again, after he received his due, the

young brave turned to the others. To Butters' dismay they showed no sign of getting bored of this game and many had begun to dismount and wander about the wagons. He grew more and more anxious. Where were McCann and Harrington? What was taking them so long? And what was happening with Weston? *Even Frank Giles would be a welcome sight at this stage*, he thought.

He stole a look along the prairie but all he saw were shadowy figures. A dusty haze lay on the plain. He had his own family to look after, anyhow. Weston was well capable of watching out for himself.

Three braves walked right up to Butters. His hand tightened on his rifle although they were so close now that the Winchester wouldn't be much use at close quarters. He still clung to it, however, like a crutch to give him a measure of hope and support. He noted the deep, rich tone of their skin, honed by days and nights outdoors.

These men were at one with nature, with their surroudings and their environment, and this thought intimidated him. He was a long way from home and he now felt that distance, every mile of it, weigh upon his shoulders. He began to regret ever setting out with his prairie schooner.

The young brave's face broke into a leer. 'Liquor,' he demanded.

Again, Butters heard Maria going to get the young Sioux what he asked for, but this time he turned to her. 'No, Maria,' he said. 'We've given enough.'

The stone certainty in his voice cut dead any argument Maria might have made.

'No!' he said to the Indian. 'No liquor.'

The smile slipped slowly from the brave's face. 'Liquor,' he said again, his voice harsher this time.

'No way, friend,' Butters replied. 'You ain't getting no liquor from me.'

The other Sioux crowded around Butters, forming an ever-tightening cordon. Where initially there'd been mischief in their eyes, there now was malevolence and violence.

He stood his ground. 'Maria,' he called, fighting to control his voice. 'Get everyone into the wagon.'

'We should go into *our* wagon, Maria,' Betty Harrington said quickly. Maria was about to disagree but then she realised that the urgency in Betty's voice might carry a greater significance. They moved away toward the Harringtons' wagon, dragging Kit Giles, Angie McCann and the children with them. None of the Sioux followed. At least not yet.

Betty scurried ahead with Kit and Angie and Maria followed closely behind, her outstretched hands ushering her two children on. Betty pushed Kit and Angie into the wagon and climbed up after them. She then helped Maria and her two children up into the crowded space. As soon as the others were all in Betty stepped out.

'Betty?' Maria enquired nervously.

'Just mind your children, Maria,' Betty whispered. 'I'll be back in a minute.'

As Betty walked away from the wagon, she pulled the revolver out from its concealment in the folds of her dress. She fought hard to control her nerves as she pulled back the hammer. Ahead, she saw Walt Butters being knocked to the ground and his rifle kicked away from him. A brave stood over him, his knife drawn. Even from where she stood, she glimpsed death in his eyes.

*Keep calm, Betty*, she thought. *You've fired this thing plenty of times at home.* She didn't allow herself to think of the fact that it was usually cans, or rabbits at the very most, that she shot at. The gun was heavy in her hand and as she raised it she felt the strain in her arm. She had to do this! She'd never forgive herself if Walt was killed and she stood by and did nothing to help him. She wouldn't see a family broken up. She couldn't bear the thought of those two young children not having a father. She was just a few yards away now and she slid her finger onto the trigger.

Seconds later, the sound of a single shot filled the air, sending the Sioux crouching for cover.

★ ★ ★

Weston saw the four Sioux surround Rose and Will. They'd grabbed the reins from them both, preventing them from getting away. Weston was closing fast, however. He gripped his mount's reins in one hand and his Colt in the other.

He saw Rose drop from her horse onto the ground and, a moment later, the same happening to Will. Once on the ground, they'd have much less chance of escape. Weston thought about firing a shot but decided against it. In all the confusion, he might hit Rose. Also, he was aware that they were greatly out-numbered, taking the Sioux back at the wagons into account.

One of the braves turned to face him.

Weston's arm flashed out and he smashed the butt of the Colt into the Indi-an's chin, knocking him to the ground. The other three turned to face him as he rode into the middle of them. Two had already dismounted and held Rose and Will tightly. Weston's unexpected arrival caused confusion among the braves. The hoof of Weston's horse slammed down on the foot of the young Sioux holding Will. Shrieking in agony, the Indian let go of Will and sank to the ground.

Will seized his opportunity and ran. He didn't break stride as he sprinted across the open prairie toward freedom. Rose just watched his back as he raced away. Will didn't once turn, just kept running.

'Let her go!' Weston growled. Two Sioux were still unharmed, one standing and one mounted. He levelled his Colt at the man holding Rose. Weston saw the fear in her eyes. The mounted Sioux wheeled his horse around beside Rose, leaned over and lifted her up across his pony's neck. Weston quickly changed his aim.

Tears flowed down Rose's face. 'No!' she cried softly as she struggled against the Indian.

Weston's finger tightened on the trigger. He had the man in his sights. The sound of a single shot filled the air.

* * *

McCann and Chet rode swiftly away from the wagons. Chet could only hope that Butters and Giles could hold out long enough and that they would return in time. They had to convince the chief to call off the attack; it was their only hope, according to Weston. Chet just hoped that they weren't harassing the wagon on the chief's orders because if they were, they would probably all die out here in the middle of nowhere. But Weston had been right about most things so far. Chet prayed that he could be right once more.

They closed in on the Indian camp. Chet saw seven tepees ahead, their triangular outlines cutting into the horizon. Children ran around, playing their games, while women went about their chores. As they drew closer Chet noted that they were being watched. Five Sioux, older than those who had ridden to the wagon train, stood at the edge of the camp, their gaze fixed on him and Emmet.

Chet reined in his horse and dismounted before these men.

'Chief. Need to speak to the chief,' Chet said rapidly.

The nearest Sioux showed no sign of understanding but it was obvious that Chet's anxiousness unsettled them. Chet repeated his request.

The children stopped running now and instead began to stare with obvious curiosity at the two strange men. The women stood silent, watching. They edged toward Chet and Emmet, surrounding them. Chet frantically pointed toward the wagons.

'Trouble. Your men . . .' he said.

There was no change in the stony expressions of the men.

'This is useless,' Emmet barked. 'I'm going back.'

'Wait,' Chet shouted. He saw a figure approaching. It was an older man and the braves stepped aside to let him pass. He stared up at Chet, his lined face revealing the toll the sun had taken on his tough skin. 'What?' he asked. His voice was deep and resonant.

Again, Chet pointed behind him, toward the camp and explained why they had come, complete with hand actions. The chief looked at him impassively for a moment before turning and walking away. He said something and the rest of the group followed him.

'Told you this was a waste of time,' Emmet said. He turned his horse without waiting for a reply from Chet and began to gallop back to the wagons.

Chet's heart sank. He'd done as Weston asked. Maybe he didn't know everything after all? Maybe Giles was right. An image of Betty flashed across his mind. She might be dead by now. He remounted and began the ride back to the wagons after Emmet, terrified of what he might find there.

He'd gone just a few yards when he heard the sound of hoofs behind him. The sound grew louder and louder. He turned in his saddle to see the source of the noise but the sun blinded him. All he saw were indistinct shapes, quickly drawing closer. As they passed him, his jaw dropped open. It was the rest of the Sioux, led by their chief, a shotgun in his hand. They quickly overtook Emmet, too, and soon after Chet heard the report of a gunshot.

★ ★ ★

Butters was on the ground, flat on his back, a knife to his throat. *This is the end*, he thought. No great feeling of peace filled him; no thoughts of an afterlife occupied his final seconds. All he could taste was the dry dust and all he could feel was the cold steel against his skin.

The face of the brave was close. Butters smelled his breath; saw the intent in those dark eyes.

He was dead, he was sure of it. Wrong place at the wrong time. As simple as that. He had met a brave determined to prove himself. He closed his eyes and thought of his family. This was the end. The chief levelled his shotgun. Even though he was travelling at quite a pace, he knew he couldn't miss. His finger squeezed the trigger and the gun bucked, firing its small lead pellets into the crowd before him. The unexpected noise caused some to crouch in terror while the sting of the lead caused others to crumple to the ground in agony.

For Walt Butters, it meant a chance of salvation.

He heard a shot and felt the knife move away from his neck. He opened his eyes and saw his attacker standing over him but looking in the other direction, the knife still in his hand. He still wasn't safe however; the stiff grimace on the brave's face told him that. Butters hadn't a clue who had fired the shot but he had to take advantage of the situation anyway.

He rose to his feet.

The brave saw him out of the corner of his eye and lunged, a primal yell coming from somewhere deep within. He would not be denied his kill.

Butters recoiled and then another shot rang out. This time, the brave fell to the ground, thumping against the hard surface.

As the Indian lay at his feet, Butters turned.

Betty Harrington stood stock still, a smoking revolver in her hand.

The first shot offered Weston his opportunity. The grip on Rose's shoulder had been loosened, the shock of the shot surprising her captor. Weston geed his horse forward and smashed his fist into the Indian's face. The brave dropped to the ground and Rose slid off the pony. Weston put himself between the two remaining Indians and Rose. He felt the blood coursing through his veins, felt the excitement of the violence. The feeling that he was now in control exhilarated him. His reflexes felt sharp, as if he was ready for anything.

This was what he was best at. What he was born to do. But then he felt the soft form of Rose behind him, smelled the delicate aroma of her soap and he wasn't so sure any more. He banished these thoughts, however. They still were not safe.

Another shot rang out and this time the battered Sioux took flight. They mounted their horses, even those hurt having gathered up enough strength to move, and galloped off over the prairie.

Weston watched them go. He heard the sound of Rose sobbing behind him. He hastily dismounted, gently lifted her onto his horse and then climbed up behind her. He held her close as they rode back toward the wagons, leading Rose's horse by its reins.

She was like a rag doll on the saddle before him, limp and lifeless. He had to hold her steady and grip the reins with one hand while guiding the loose horse with his other. She'd been through an ordeal, and he could only hope that she would recover from it. He'd seen it before, people ruined and destroyed by incidents such as this. But Rose was strong, he believed.

The Sioux around the wagons had moved off also. A cold shiver ran through him, however. There was a body lying prone on the ground. Had he done the right thing? He'd truly thought that the best chance to avoid inflaming the situation was by going to speak with the chief. After all, it had worked for him before. Admittedly, the barrel of his Colt had been jammed under the chief's chin at the time.

He rode into camp and Emmet McCann ran to them, his arms outstretched. Rose half-fell and half-slid down the side of Weston's horse and into her father's arms. Out of the corner of his eye, Weston spotted Will, Kit and Frank Giles embracing also. Frank must have ridden after Will as he ran across the plain, away from the Sioux. Whatever he felt about the Giles men, he didn't want to see either of them killed. Not yet anyway.

The Sioux had retreated to their camp, all except the chief and a couple of braves. They stood over the dead body of their companion.

Chet came over to Weston and quickly explained what had happened.

'Didn't know Betty had it in her,'

Weston said.

'Me, neither,' Chet replied, pride in his voice.

'You did good, too, Chet.'

He just bowed his head.

'I mean it.' To Weston's surprise, he felt as if he really did mean it. This group of people had done something to him. Something he couldn't define. The lone wolf was beginning to enjoy running with this pack.

Weston left Chet and walked over to the chief. They had raised the body from the ground and placed it across the saddle of one of the horses.

'Sorry,' Weston said.

The chief looked intently at him. 'Young...' he said, gesturing toward the dead man, '...and stupid.' All the while he kept his eye on Weston. 'Me,' he pointed at his chest, 'no trouble.'

Weston nodded. 'I don't want any trouble either.'

The Sioux rode slowly away, guiding the horse with the dead brave between them. Weston watched them disappear into the distance, their silhouettes etched into the horizon.

# 10

Pete and Joe were ready and waiting when Bogue left the hotel and rode out of town. There weren't many folks up and about at that early hour so they had to hang back to stay undetected. Bogue took the trail westward at a steady pace.

*Hopefully taking us to the feller that robbed the bank*, Pete thought.

Pete and Joe exchanged barely a word for the first few hours, concentrating on keeping Bogue in their sights.

At last, Joe broke the silence. 'So, who exactly is this Dan Bogue?'

Pete knew that Joe was bound to have asked this question at some stage. Joe trusted him, he had no doubt about that, but he was not one for following orders blindly. He had avoided bringing up how he knew Bogue for a reason, however. Because every time he thought about it, those terrible memories returned. He knew that he had to tell Joe, though. He owed him that much, at least.

'Dan Bogue,' he began, 'is originally from Arizona. He was an Indian hunter. When the war began he offered his skills to the Confederates. He quickly became recognized as an expert scout, helping his militia stalk and kill Yankees before disappearing into the night; that kind of thing. But he had no loyalty to Rebel or Yankee. He saw the war as a way of making money, simple as that. His sense of danger was uncanny. He escaped from tight situations many times, bringing his fellow soldiers with him. He was a model soldier, as long as he received his eleven dollars a month.

'But then it became apparent that the tide was turning, that the Rebels were not going to be successful. And, more importantly, the money began to dry up. That was when he made a decision, and it was not a difficult one for a man like Dan Bogue. He slipped away from his unit one night and sought out the Union lines. He slit the throat of a Yankee soldier and stole his uniform. He then made himself known to the commanding officer of the group and passed himself off as a Yankee escaped from a band of Rebel guerrillas. To prove his story, he led the Yankees to the Rebel band and watched as they cut them down in their sleep.

'He left his old comrades dead and dying on that cold, damp forest floor. He had seen no future with the Confederate cause so he had switched sides. It was as simple as that.'

'How do you know all this?' Joe asked.

Pete wasn't sure he could answer that question. He felt as if he had a rock jammed in his throat. 'Because,' he said at last, 'one man survived that attack. Although his injuries were so severe that he died soon after the war ended.'

Joe waited for him to continue.

'That man was Mike Baker, my brother.'

★ ★ ★

143

It was late afternoon by the time the town of Lawrence came into Dan Bogue's sight, its wooden buildings stark against the prairie. He hadn't fully thought out his plan of action, but he knew at least that he must be careful. He'd passed through Baxter Springs undetected but Lawrence might be a different story. In a big town strangers could pass relatively unnoticed; in a smaller town like Lawrence, an unfamiliar face was likely to get more attention. So, no lawmen this time. He would have to change tack.

The buildings in Lawrence were a mixture of old and new, a legacy of the raid on the town some years before by Quantrill and his band of guerrillas that had devastated the place. Lawrence had recovered, however, and now conducted business just as any other town its size. He moseyed slowly down the main street before pulling up at a water trough.

He dismounted and allowed his horse to drink deeply. He splashed some water on his face and ran his hands through his hair. He took a good look around. There weren't many people on the main stem. He pulled his mount along as he strolled purposefully down the street, swivelling his head slowly and almost imperceptibly from left to right.

He kept moving until he heard the sound of a piano playing up ahead. *A piano being played badly*, he thought. He hitched his horse to the railing outside the saloon. The door was wide open, allowing him a clear view. He stepped up onto the wooden boardwalk and went inside. With one glance he took in all the detail of what lay before him. This was the saloon McGraw had told him about: the Kansas Belle.

The interior consisted of a long counter on the right-hand side of the room with the rest of the space taken up by a series of tables and booths. The piano was near to the door so that the music would carry out and attract passers-by. The bar was busy enough for that time of the evening, maybe five drinkers at the counter and most of the ten tables and booths had at least one person sitting at them.

The piano was being played by an elderly man, whose pay was obviously in liquid form, and beside him, singing at the top of her lungs, was a woman Bogue would bet wasn't as drunk as she let on.

He sidled up to the bar and slipped onto a stool. He ordered a beer and a whiskey and downed the beer first in one swallow and sent the whiskey the same way immediately after. He then called for the same again.

'You sure are thirsty, stranger,' came a voice from along the bar.

Bogue looked to his left toward the source of the hail. Three dingy-looking men stared at him, sneers on their faces and hardness in their eyes. He'd seen these types in every saloon he had ever entered. Fellers that thought they owned the place just because they spent so much time in there, killing themselves with whiskey while the weeds covered their farms. They felt that they had to pry into everyone's business, living vicariously through other people's experiences because they'd long ago sacrificed their own to the barstool. And it was this particular trait that Bogue intended to exploit.

\* \* \*

'What do you suppose he wants here?' Joe asked as they rode into town.

'Don't know,' Pete muttered. 'But I sure hope the lawmen in Lawrence would have told us if our bank robber was hiding out here.'

'They've had enough trouble themselves, what with that shoot-out and all,' Joe replied.

Pete just nodded. He had read about it in the newspaper but hadn't thought it connected to the robbery. He was beginning to have second thoughts now, however.

'Should we go see the marshal?' Joe asked.

'And tell him what?' Pete asked. 'That we're following Dan Bogue around their town? I think we'd better keep ourselves to ourselves here, and watch Bogue from a distance. I feel like we may be reaching the end of our trail.'

They watched Bogue enter the saloon. 'Let's go across the road,' Pete said, 'so's we can get a good view of what's going on.'

They dismounted outside a saloon across the street from the Kansas Belle. Not directly opposite, for fear of being spotted. Pete was confident that they were out of Bogue's line of sight. They took seats just inside the window, with a clear view across the street. If Dan Bogue left that building, they'd be after him in an instant.

★ ★ ★

Bogue stared at the three men. 'It's hot travelling out there,' he said, and did his best to crack a smile. Best to let them think they're in charge on their own territory, he thought, and lull them into a false sense of superiority.

'Sure is,' one of them replied. He was a hard-faced man, with a thick moustache and a few days' stubble on his face. His hair stood out from his head at all angles, obviously not having seen a brush or comb for many a day, if ever. The two men with him seemed content with letting him do the talking. He was the lead dog, it seemed. The others just stared at Bogue with their vacant sneers, all the while getting more and more drunk.

'Where you travelling from?' the man asked.

'Baxter Springs,' Bogue replied. 'Name's Crean, Adam Crean,' he said.

'Pat Giles.'

'What you drinking, Pat? And you two as well?'

'That's mighty generous of you. We'll have the same as you, three beers and three whiskies.'

Bogue didn't flinch. 'Make it four,' he said to the barman.

'What are you doing in Lawrence?' Giles asked. 'You come all this way to see our small town? You know, I was in Baxter Springs once. Too many people. Didn't like it at all.'

The drunk beside him muttered, 'Too many people,' in agreement. 'I agree. And no good saloons, either. Not like this place!'

This brought a small cheer from the men and was quickly drowned out by another jarring note from the piano.

'You planning on staying in town for a while or just passing through?' Giles asked.

'Not sure. Got some business to do here, look at some cattle. Not sure I'll stay long, though.'

'Why not?'

'Well . . .' Bogue shrugged his shoulders.

'No, come on,' Giles urged, slurring his words as he got worked up. 'Tell us what's wrong with our town.' His voice had grown louder now, catching the attention of some of the other patrons. This was not what Bogue had planned. He hadn't bargained on being the focus of the whole saloon . . . Time to cut to the chase, he decided.

'Well, I just heard that some fellers got

150

shot up here recently. That's all.'

'Ha!' Giles exclaimed wearily. 'That's all everyone's talking about in this town. I hoped an outsider like you might have something more interesting to say for yourself.'

He turned away from Bogue and resumed his drinking. Bogue knew that he would have to keep him talking or he would have bought all that liquor for no purpose. He was sure that this nosy loudmouth was his best chance of finding out information and he wasn't about to give up easily.

'It's just that people don't have the same version of the story. Everyone I talk to has a different idea of what hap. pened. Maybe you could tell me what really happened? I figure if anyone would know the story, you would. You look like an intelligent feller.'

This was a blatant appeal to Giles' vanity. He faced Bogue once more and gestured to the barman, never once taking his eyes off of Bogue. 'Same again, all round.'

The barman looked at Bogue, who gave him a quick nod.

'It happened about a week ago,' Giles began. 'We were all sitting here as usual, minding our own business. Two men were sitting around a table, over there,' he jerked his thumb toward the back of the room. 'And they seemed to be getting along all friendly-like, until one of them started shouting. Calling the other a cheat and a liar. Shouting something about wanting his money back. Now, the feller still sitting down, his name was Josiah Maxwell, Bat Maxwell's son.' He stopped and looked directly at Bogue. 'You know who Bat Maxwell is?'

*That man again*, he thought. *He couldn't seem to get away from him. Best to play dumb.*

Bogue shook his head.

'You don't know who Bat Maxwell is?' Giles asked incredulously.

'Never heard of him,' Bogue lied.

'He's a very important man. Owns a lot of land around here. He even bought some of it,' Giles said knowingly.

Bogue decided he had better play along or he'd never get to the end of Giles' story. He felt weary. The travelling; the role-playing; it had all taken its toll and now that he'd had a few drinks, he just wanted it all to end. Wanted to get Pat Giles out of his face and to move on. Wanted to go and get Weston and collect his money. He was getting a bad feeling about this job. But the lure of the money meant that he continued playing his part and egged Giles on.

'What do you mean?' he asked.

Giles lowered his voice for effect. 'He's a land baron. Stole most everything he owns. An expert claim-jumper. The war was the best thing that ever happened to Bat Maxwell. Many fellers came home to find him on their land. He has a small army of outlaws to do his dirty work for him and enough money to keep the law off his back. He has two sons. Or one, now I suppose, since that Josiah ain't with us no longer. I shouldn't be telling you this, might get myself into trouble.'

Bogue knew that he was angling for

another drink but chose to ignore the hint. 'So, what were young Maxwell and this man arguing about?'

'Don't know that, I'm afraid,' Giles replied, 'but all of a sudden it got real messy. The jigger pulled his piece and started firing at Josiah. Blew his insides out. Maxwell had another feller with him but he out-drew him, as well. He made for the back door as two other fellers, Maxwell's folk, too, I reckon, came in the front. They all disappeared off into the night. Maxwell's men came back later. No sign of the killer. It's like he was a ghost or something. Strangest thing I've ever heard of. Most reckon he must be dead.'

'Why?' Bogue asked.

'Simple. Nobody kills Bat Maxwell's son and gets away with it.'

Bogue stared directly into Giles' eyes, eventually making him turn away.

'But you reckon differently, don't you?' Bogue said.

A coy smile crossed Giles' face. 'Maybe I do, maybe I don't.'

'You reckon differently, or you *know* differently?'

'I'm pretty sure, and I might tell you what I know if you offer me the right price.'

Bogue sized him up. Giles was definitely drunk but his eyes now possessed a clarity that hadn't been present before. What he was telling him, he believed was true.

Whether it actually was the truth or not was another matter, but Bogue felt that he couldn't let this opportunity pass by. 'How much?'

Giles gave a little nod. 'I knew you were an intelligent feller when you walked in the door.' He smiled triumphantly. 'See, I know people. I can size them up. Know what they want, and know how to get the right price for it.'

Bogue was growing tired of all this talking. 'And what is that price?'

Giles gave a surreptitious look around. Everyone else in the bar was safely encased in their warm fug of comfortable drunkenness. 'Let's go outside. I don't want to do business in here.'

They left the saloon and Bogue followed Giles down the alleyway next to it. The saloon and the building beside it were built close together, and the roofs of the worn structures almost touched each other, casting a dark shadow on the alley.

'One hundred dollars,' Giles said defiantly, 'for what I know.'

Bogue, sick of Giles by now, handed him the money. 'Talk,' he said simply.

'My brother is on a wagon train, heading west toward Fort Laramie. He wrote me, told me that they found a feller out cold on the plain just outside of town on the night of the shooting.'

'That's a coincidence,' Bogue replied. 'Could be anyone.'

Giles looked crestfallen. 'No,' he said, hurt in his voice. 'It's him. I know it.'

Bogue looked at him doubtfully. 'I don't suppose your brother told you his name?'

'He mentioned a name, all right,' he said tentatively.

156

'Get it right and you just might get to keep your money.' It was evident from Bogue's tone of voice that he wasn't playing games. He lowered his head in thought.

'I could get you the letter,' he said. 'It's back on my farm, not far from here.'

'How about you think some more first. I don't feel like travelling any more today.'

Giles' forehead creased as he thought deeply, trying desperately to dredge the name from the recesses of his memory. The drink couldn't help, Bogue thought as he studied the man's pained expression, muddying the pathways in his mind and slowing down his thoughts.

'It wasn't a common name,' he mumbled.

Bogue sighed deeply, finding it harder and harder to restrain himself. His hand instinctively went toward his holster on his hip.

'I nearly have it,' Giles said, creasing his forehead even tighter. He looked up suddenly at Bogue. He had the name.

'Weston,' he said. 'He said his name was Weston.'

A thin smile crossed Bogue's lips. 'I was hoping you'd say that.'

Giles didn't see the butt of Bogue's gun come crashing down on the side of his head, knocking him unconscious.

Bogue reached down to the prone body and relieved him of the money. As an afterthought he threw twenty dollars down. He walked out of the shadowed laneway with a renewed sense of purpose. He was finally on the right track.

# 11

Pete jumped to his feet when he saw Bogue emerge from the saloon accompanied by a rather dishevelled-looking companion. He nudged Joe's arm. 'There he is. Let's see where they go.'

He watched as the two men entered the alleyway. He couldn't know for definite that Bogue would come back out of there but he didn't see any value in trailing him too closely. One thing in their favour was the fact that Bogue's horse remained tethered to the rail in front of the saloon. Unless he stole another one, he wouldn't be leaving town any time soon.

He fought to control his breathing; it seemed like his heart was set to burst from his chest. This waiting, this inaction, and the tension it brought with it seemed set to overwhelm him. What was he doing here, anyway? That was a question that kept coming back to him. Why wasn't he at home with his wife and baby?

Deep down, he knew the answer. He had come to reclaim some part of himself, a part that Mayor Dell had taken away. He had to rediscover the man he once was.

Then he could return, proud and worthy of Dorothy and Tom. But in order to do that, he would have to find the bank robber. And right now all his hopes were pinned on Dan Bogue.

Bogue emerged from the alleyway and Pete's breath whistled through his teeth in relief. He waited for the other man who had entered the alleyway with him to come into view but wasn't surprised when he didn't. Bogue mounted up and rode slowly down the street. Town was getting busy, the fine evening bringing people out for a stroll, some food or a few drinks.

'Let's stay on foot,' Pete told Joe. 'I don't think he's going far.'

They spent the next hour following Bogue around Lawrence, always keeping a discreet distance, their feelings of astonishment growing more acute as they watched his behaviour. Or, more specifically, his purchases.

'I don't know about you,' Joe said eventually, 'but I'm getting mighty worried.'

'I'd have to agree with you,' Pete replied. 'I think we may be going further than Lawrence.'

'Certainly looks like it.'

'How much money you got?' Pete asked.

Joe turned out his pockets, revealing little more than a few dollars and a lot of lint.

'Better than nothing,' Pete muttered. He had a little cash on him also. 'Keep an eye on Bogue as best you can. I'll meet you back at our horses in one hour or as close to it as possible. If he leaves town, let him go. He can't travel fast with that load.' They split up and went about their business.

Just over an hour later, Pete marched a heavily laden mule down the main street to where Joe stood waiting. 'I didn't

161

think you'd be able to get one at such short notice,' Joe said.

Pete smiled. He could hear the reluctance and anxiety in Joe's voice. He was in no doubt that Joe had hoped that his scheme would have fallen through. He was sure that if he had his way, Joe would ride out right now and arrest Dan Bogue and be done with him. But Pete didn't believe that would bring them any closer to the bank robber. In his mind it was this way or not at all.

'You don't have to come along if you don't want to,' Pete said. 'I know you're not totally convinced by this whole thing.' He waved his hand to encompass the mule and their two horses.

Joe looked up at his friend. 'Pete,' he said, 'if you say that we need to do this, then that's good enough for me. Always was and always will be.'

Pete couldn't hide the smile that crossed his face. In truth, he wasn't sure he could carry on without Joe. Now he just hoped that he'd bought enough supplies for them both.

'Bogue left town?' Pete asked.

Joe nodded.

'Down the trail?' Again, Joe nodded.

'Well then, let's get going.'

They mounted up and Pete pulled their heavily laden mule along.

'California, here we come,' Joe said quietly.

* * *

Bogue had set off with his horse and mule about thirty minutes ahead of Pete and Joe. He headed northwest, aiming to join up with the overland trail somewhere along the Great Platte River Road. He wasn't sure how far behind the wagon train he was, but he was confident that he could make up a lot of time. Also, since he wasn't encumbered by oxen, his horse and mule should make better time.

He crossed the Kansas River by ferry before heading for the Blue River, the first of eighteen streams he must cross before reaching the Platte. This part of the journey was difficult travelling, mainly through tall grass interspersed with trees. This country contained game aplenty. Wolves howled at night and skulked by day, just out of rifle range. Antelopes were also spotted, again just out of range, their budlike horns and white throats barely visible above the top of the grass, peering eagerly with their round, black eyes at Bogue and his horse and mule. Crows, ravens, turkey buzzards and grey owls were regular companions. By day, the birds' raucous calls mingled with the hum of bees, grasshoppers and locusts, while the usual sounds of night were the whining of mosquitoes and the bellowing, croaking and trilling of frogs from marshier ground.

Bogue travelled well for the first two days, and then the Platte came into view.

The banks of the Platte were lined by a thin fringe of timber, the only trees on the horizon now that he had left behind the dense groves of tall green hardwood. On the other side of the river, a broad, well-defined trail led westward across the plains, following the wide yet shallow Platte into dusty, arid territory but promising at least the prospect of easy going. The barren wastes of the river valley stretched before him: level plains, measureless to the eye, soft green hills and hollows patchily covered by thin groves of trees. It was here that Dan Bogue decided to stop and wait.

He moved into a thin stretch of trees and unloaded his things. He was being followed, he was certain of it, and he cursed himself. If he'd been asked how he knew, he couldn't easily articulate an answer. Some instinct told him he was being tracked, hunted maybe. He was familiar enough with the role of being the tracker to know that he had to make a stand and take some definite action if he wasn't to be surprised further down the trail.

He'd been careless; there was no escaping that fact. He had let his guard down. Although he was loath to admit it, he'd been distracted by the money, by the challenge, and by the excitement of it all. That was most unlike him; that kind of behaviour could get a man killed.

He had no idea who was after him. Maybe there was a price on his own head? Maybe it was Charlie Weston tracking him down? This thought briefly brought a smile before he settled back to wait.

# 12

After their encounter with the Sioux, the wagon train made good progress to Fort Laramie. The fort's fifteen-foot tall adobe walls loomed before the wagons. A wooden palisade ran around the fort and the entrance with its square earthen tower with embrasures and loopholes was offset by the Black Hills in the near foreground and Laramie Peak in the background.

They'd arrived at the busy trading post battered but unbowed, with all those who set out still alive. This was a major waypoint on their journey and a sense of achievement filled the emigrants.

As the wagoners entered they saw that the housing was primitive, with small apartments, each with a door and a window opening onto the main courtyard. But, after the trail, anything resembling a house was a welcome sight. Here was a chance to buy provisions, wash clothes, use the smithy to shoe horses and repair wagon wheels, and generally rest and recuperate, and it was with gusto and euphoria that the overlanders set up camp next to the fort.

But they were grievously disappointed at the meagre range of goods available and the astronomical prices. Many items were unobtainable and those that could be bought — coffee, brown sugar, flour, powder, lead, percussion caps and calico — were at a premium, much to the disgust of the would-be purchasers.

Weston now had a decision to make. Would he stay with the emigrants or would he return to his old way of life? He hadn't spoken much to Rose since he rescued her. She spent most of her time with her parents. She was recovering, healing, he believed. This return to civilisation, however, even though Fort Laramie was a remote outpost, served to jolt Weston into making up his mind. An experience like Rose had suffered took time to get over. He would leave her be. It would be easier that way.

He walked over to Chet, who sat beside his wagon. 'I won't be continuing with you,' he confided. His voice was low and grave. He hadn't taken this decision lightly.

'We'll miss you,' Chet replied.

Weston now considered Chet his friend. At least as close to a friend as he'd ever known, and he was grateful that he didn't challenge him on his decision.

'Thanks, Chet. You'll be fine. There are other wagons here that are going the same way as you. You'll all be OK together.'

'What are you going to do?'

'I'll figure something out,' he muttered. 'Tell the others that I said goodbye.'

'You're not going to do it yourself?' Chet asked, surprise in his tone.

'No. I'd rather just leave.'

'Wait a second.'

'Look, Chet,' Weston replied wearily.

'I want to give you something.'

'There's no need. You saved my life, you don't owe me anything.'

'We owe you everything,' Chet replied.

'Take my saddle-horse. And be careful. We hope to see you again sometime.'

Weston didn't reply, as he was unable to articulate his thanks. He rode out of Fort Laramie that night with a heavy heart, not sure what might lie ahead.

★  ★  ★

The morning after they arrived, Rose woke early and wandered excitedly around Fort Laramie. As she walked, her thoughts turned to Weston. He provoked all sorts of feelings within her. Feelings that Will Giles certainly did not stir up. Weston was a real man. He'd been places, done exciting things. Heck, he'd been the cause of more excitement in the few days that she'd known him than she'd had in her whole lifetime up to that point. Sure, he was older than her. And he had barely spoken two words together to her, but she had seen him watching her. He thought that she hadn't, but he was wrong. There was something there, some connection, she was sure of it.

But, being Emmet McCann's girl, she also had a streak of sensibility running through her. She'd wait and see. The remainder of the trip would tell her a lot more about Weston.

Everyone was up and about when she returned to the wagons. Food was cooking and tantalising smells filled the air. She hailed her father as she drew near. He returned the greeting but quickly turned away from her.

* * *

Emmet didn't know what to say to Rose. He had mixed feelings about the whole situation. He knew that his daughter was a very attractive girl. He'd seen plenty eyeing her up over the last few years, not an easy thing for a man his age to cope with.

This was the first time she had ever given any indication of interest in someone, however. They had seen the way she was around him. Weston was a tough man, older than Rose by a good number of years but still a young enough man all the same. And he had saved their lives out on the trail, Emmet reasoned. He couldn't be all bad, even if there was something inside him, some motivation driving him onward that Emmet couldn't quite decipher.

When he looked at Weston, he always got the feeling that there was far more going on behind those coal-black eyes than he could ever understand. It was this reserve, this secrecy that worried Emmet. He wasn't entirely sure that Weston would be suitable for his daughter. Not that Weston, or Rose for that matter, had come to him about the subject or anything like it.

It was tough on Will Giles, he conceded. Following her about like a puppy dog only to be abandoned when Weston came along. At least one thing was for sure, Emmet thought, she would have been safe with Weston. He would never have allowed anything to happen to her. But now this was all idle speculation, anyway.

'Hey Pa,' she called cheerily to him, 'what's happening?' He looked across at his wife. Angie knew all that Emmet had been thinking. They held no secrets from each other. Their daughter was their greatest achievement, they believed, their whole world. They hated to see her hurt.

Angie stood beside her husband. They had to tell her, she would be hurt, they knew that, though she might not show it. She was stubborn, like her father. They respected her too much to treat her like a child. To act as if they knew what was best for her. Emmet had to admit, and it was tough for him to do so, that his little girl was now a grown woman. She had a mind of her own and he couldn't keep hiding her away from the world out there. Bad things happened. That was life. For those very reasons, they must tell her.

'Rose,' Angie began. The expression on her daughter's face changed.

'What is it? Are you all right? Are you sick?'

Somehow, Emmet was gladdened to hear her so worried after their health. She was always going to be his little girl, of that he was certain.

'No, dear, we're both fine. It's something else.'

'Well?' she asked expectantly. 'Is it Auntie Eve? Did you get some news from home?'

'No.' Emmet shook his head.

'Just tell her,' Angie said softly.

'Tell me what?' Rose's voice was barely audible as the words left her lips.

Emmet took a deep breath and delivered his news. 'It's Weston,' he said quietly but distinctly. 'He's left.'

Rose's mouth trembled and Emmet thought she was going to faint but she quickly regained her composure.

'How do you mean?' she asked.

'He told Chet he was leaving and he disappeared last night. Quit Fort Laramie altogether.'

'What are you telling me for?' She didn't give her father time to answer. 'What do I care about that brute anyway?

He's nothing more than a liability to us. We'd never have gotten to California with him. I'm glad he's gone.' Emmet heard her words but he knew from the pain in her eyes that she was lying. He reached out to her as she turned to walk away. She either didn't see his gesture or else chose to ignore it as she strode away from the wagons.

'Rose,' he called after her.

Angie put her hand on her husband's shoulder. 'Leave her be,' she said. 'She just needs some time.'

'I don't like her wandering about here by herself,' he replied. 'It's dangerous. Lots of strange folk.' There was an edge to his voice, sharpened by worry for her. For his little girl.

'She's able to take care of herself,' Angie replied. 'Leave her be for the time being. She'll come back.' Angie left Emmet standing alone, looking forlornly after his daughter.

★ ★ ★

Rose's feet pounded the earth as she left the wagons behind. She wasn't sure who she was angrier with; Weston for leaving, or her father for assuming she cared. Her anger subsided as she walked, however, and gave way to her true emotions. She stopped and leaned against the wall of an adobe hut, physically drained by her grief.

*Weston has left the train.*

The words went off like gunshots in her head. All she thought she knew, all the ideas she had in her head of what might lie ahead for her had just disappeared. Leaving behind her fears that she was a husk of a young woman with no achievements and no real purpose. She'd never loved before, only ever worked at home on the farm and even then her doting father had taken it easy on her. She'd never really had any responsibilities, although she always tried to do her best for her parents. She felt as if she was living a life unfulfilled.

Most girls were married at her age but she seemed to exist in a world of her own, cut off from real society. She felt a flash of anger toward her parents for making her life like this but that anger quickly passed. She was an only child. An only female child, to make matters worse. It was no wonder that her parents doted on her. She'd been made aware from a very young age that they considered her a blessing from heaven, coming as she did after they had almost given up the idea of having any children. In return, she did her best to make them proud of her. Did her best never to upset them, never to go out of her way to make their lives difficult or to make them worry. But now she seemed to be suffering the consequences of never having pushed herself. This journey, this migration, was the most exciting thing she had ever participated in. She hoped it was going to be a life-altering experience. A journey that would endow her life with some form and meaning.

The reality of her situation, that she was stuck in this fort, far from home and far from their destination also, struck her hard. She questioned what she was doing and why. Why had Weston made such an impression on her? She could not express why he caught her eye.

Maybe, she thought, it would now make it easier to forget that he had ever been there. Maybe he would slip out of her mind as easily as he entered it. Deep down, she knew that this would not be the case, however. She walked around the fort for a couple of minutes before she returned to the wagons.

The first thing she did when she returned was to fall into her father's arms and the second was to tear up her letter to Aunt Eve and write a new one. One that bore no mention of Charlie Weston.

More news had reached Emmet McCann at this stage. Walt Butters had approached him, anger visible on his face. 'They're gone,' he said fiercely.

'I know,' Emmet replied. 'Left last night.'

Butters couldn't hide his surprise.

'You knew?' he asked, 'and you didn't think to tell us?'

McCann was a little taken aback by Butters' tone. 'Sorry, Walt,' he said, 'I was going to tell you this morning.'

Butters was obviously still angry, 'I know that we didn't always get along but we've known them for years. Maybe we could have stopped them from leaving.'

This time it was Emmet's turn to look surprised. 'I'm afraid I'm not following you,' Emmet said. 'Weston left the train last night, that's who I'm talking about.'

'Weston!' Butters shouted. He took a moment to digest this information before continuing. 'I'm talking about the Gileses. All their things are gone. They've headed back home.'

Something of a pall hung over the group that night. To lose some of their original members in such a fashion had shaken them. There was little doubt that Weston's arrival had unsettled the Gileses, especially Frank, maybe even leading to their turning back. Frank Giles was a loose cannon, prone to rashness, but he was still an old friend and neighbour. Looking back over the last few days, Emmet felt guilty about how they had immediately accepted Weston and ridden roughshod over Frank's concerns in the process.

But, as Chet reminded him, they might still be stuck on the other side of the Platte if it weren't for Weston. Or their bones might now be bleaching on the plain, victims of the marauding Sioux. Where he himself had failed, Emmet surmised, was failing to integrate Weston into the group properly while taking the Giles' concerns into account as he did so. The result now seemed to be that neither Weston nor the Giles would be travelling onward with them. Fort Laramie had certainly brought a lot of change to the wagon train.

* * *

Joe and Pete stopped at a stream and splashed cool water onto their faces to ease the effects of the afternoon sun. In their three days of travelling they'd settled into an easy routine. They generally ate in the saddle during the day, stopping to cook and have a main meal in the evening. Bogue was often out of sight, somewhere ahead on the trail, but they kept going, always assuming that they were on the right path. Occasionally they'd catch glimpses of him cresting a rise ahead or riding beneath them in a valley, always just enough to help them forget the aches and pains they suffered from being in the saddle for so many hours.

After their stop at the stream Joe called to Pete to take a look behind them. A figure on horseback slowly approached. The horseman looked as if he was in danger of slipping from his saddle. Joe and Pete looked at each other out of the corner of their eyes. They were on edge, tense from following Bogue. They were both aware that nothing might be what it seemed in this unfamiliar landscape.

'Get your gun, Joe,' Pete said quietly.

The rider was just yards away now. His hat sat askew on his head and he seemed to be barely hanging onto the reins with the tips of his fingers. Pete walked toward him, all the while scanning the horizon. A sudden movement drew his eye back to the rider. Pete instinctively reached for his holster, which he quickly realised he had left back at the stream. There was no need for a weapon, however. Lying on the ground, like a sack of grain, was the rider.

Pete jogged over and turned him onto his back. He inhaled sharply as he looked at the man's parched face. The rider's lips were cracked; it was obvious that he hadn't tasted water for quite a while. His face was dusty and a low, dull moan emanated from his throat.

'Bring some water!' Pete called.

Joe grabbed his canteen and they poured water into the man's mouth and onto his face. After a moment's pause, the stranger drank thirstily, the water gradually bringing him round.

His eyes flickered open and stared at the two men standing over him. Pete helped him up to a sitting position and handed the canteen to him. 'Don't drink too much,' Pete warned, 'or your stomach will cramp.' Ignoring him, the man raised the canteen to his lips and took a long thirsty gulp, the water visibly revitalising him.

Wiping his mouth with his sleeve, he lowered the canteen and nodded gratefully to Joe and Pete. 'Thanks,' he muttered. His voice was harsh and rough, the water not having washed all the grit out of his throat. 'You pretty much saved my life, I reckon.'

'You're in a rough state, partner,' Pete said. 'What're you doing out here all by yourself?'

The stranger waited for quite a while before answering. 'I might as well tell the truth,' he said. 'I saw you leaving Lawrence and heading out here with your mule. Figured you were either fixing to head west on your own or planning to catch up with the wagon train. Thought I might try and join you. By the time I had my supplies together I was about a day behind you.'

Pete looked at him doubtfully. 'That's all well and good, partner, except I don't see any supplies with you.'

'That's the problem,' he said. 'Indians attacked me. Caught me unawares. Took everything.'

'Kansa Indians?'

'Not sure,' the stranger replied. 'Maybe Sioux.'

Pete shot a doubtful glance at Joe.

'Look, fellers. Thank you for your help,' the stranger said. 'You don't have to believe me but I am determined to keep heading west. With or without your help. I'm sure I can shoot some buffalo, or antelope or something.' He got to his feet, tottered a little unsteadily and grabbed at Pete for support.

'We've got just about enough to help you out for a little while, feller,' Pete said. He looked the stranger straight in the face. There was no doubt that he was in rough condition and needed some help. 'Name's Pete Baker, and this here's Joe Flaherty.'

'Dave Maxwell,' the stranger said.

'Well, Dave,' Pete said, 'let's have us something to eat.'

After they had eaten bacon and beans, the three men mounted up. Little conversation passed between them as Joe and Pete struggled to make up their minds about their new travelling companion. No matter what way he thought about it, Pete didn't believe Maxwell's story about an Indian attack. The Kansa Sioux earned more money from trading and helping emigrants along the trail than by attacking them or stealing from them. It wasn't unknown for Sioux or Pawnee to attack white men, especially if travelling alone, but such attacks were rare in this area. They usually happened further along the trail. But there was no doubting that Maxwell had been in a bad state. Why was he so dishevelled? That was the question that bothered Pete.

Up ahead, the River Platte came into view, focusing their minds once more on the task in hand.

'Where are we going to cross?' Joe asked.

The three men drew nearer to the thin line of trees that bordered the Platte.

'We'll continue on,' Pete said. 'The trail doesn't cross the river until further along.'

They rode on, the river on their right.

★ ★ ★

Bogue watched them approach his hiding place. Their hats cast shadows, hid their faces. Where there'd been two riders, now there were three, he realised. No matter, he was still sure that he could handle them. They were armed, the stocks of their rifles sticking out of saddle scabbards. There was nothing unusual about them. There was no guarantee that they were following him. They showed no signs of edginess or suspicious behaviour. Something kept him back, though, hidden in the trees. Maybe it was his inherent sense of distrust, of self-preservation. Either way, he held back from making himself known.

The men drew abreast of him, all three looking toward the river. He couldn't get a clear look at them, couldn't tell if he knew them or not until one of them turned his head to the left to speak to his colleague. Bogue's breath caught for a moment before he whipped out his pistol and swung onto the trail behind the three riders.

* * *

'He must be far ahead,' Joe muttered, 'we've had no sign of him for a while.' He kept his voice low, so that Maxwell couldn't hear him.

Pete was about to reply when a voice from behind them stopped them in their tracks.

'Stop right there!'

They swung their horses round and were confronted by Bogue, his pistol levelled at them. Pete's blood ran cold. He'd been careless, preoccupied by trying to figure out Maxwell's story. He'd almost forgotten that they were trailing Bogue until Joe mentioned him. And now, here he was, as if Joe's very mention had summoned him. And he had the drop on them.

'Don't none of you reach for your guns. Keep your hands where I can see them. There's only three of you and six slugs in my gun. That's plenty, the way I can shoot. Ain't that right, Marshal? Deputy?' He nodded to Pete and Joe in turn.

Pete was in no doubt that Bogue wasn't bluffing. He'd cut them down in an instant, if he saw fit. He knew Joe wouldn't do anything foolish; he wasn't so sure about Maxwell. He now seriously regretted helping him. 'We won't cause any trouble,' he said, holding his arms out from his sides. 'Sure we won't.'

Joe copied Pete but Maxwell didn't.

Bogue drew the hammer back on his Colt. 'Don't be foolish,' he said.

Pete looked anxiously toward Maxwell. He figured that if Bogue got that trigger finger going he just might not stop until they were all dead. Maxwell was putting them all in mortal danger.

'Maxwell,' Pete said loudly, trying to penetrate the shroud that seemed to have descended on him, 'do as he says.'

Bogue's eyes flicked to Pete for a moment and then back to Maxwell.

'Maxwell?' he asked.

'That's right, Dan. Dave Maxwell, at your service.' Maxwell replied. He still had his hands by his sides, hovering near his holsters.

The two lawmen kept quiet, Pete hoping to be forgotten in the background. This plot was thickening like an old soup, and he would gladly ease out of it now, if it were only possible.

'Why are you here?' Bogue asked Maxwell. 'Your Pop not think I can get the job done?'

'Let's just say he was covering his bets,' Maxwell answered.

'What about these two fellers?' He jerked the gun barrel toward Pete and Joe. 'They in on it, too?'

'They're not with me, if that's what you mean.'

*That's gratitude for you*, Pete thought. 'Although they did help me out when I ran out of water,' Maxwell added. 'But we can't stand here like this all day,' he said to Bogue. 'We're losing ground all the time.'

Bogue just stared at him, then turned his attention to Pete. 'What's your story, Marshal? Why are you following me? If you recognized me when I called to see you, why didn't you try to arrest me then?'

Pete's mind raced. Should he come right out and tell the truth, or try to hide their true motives? The fact that Bogue was the one holding the pistol made his mind up for him. 'We're after the feller who robbed the bank. When you came around asking questions about him, we thought that you might know something. That's why we're following you, to see who you're going to lead us to.'

'What were you going to do then? Were you going to arrest us both? Kill us both?'

'I have no interest in you, Bogue,' Pete said. 'All I want is the bank robber. Then my life can get back to normal. I can go home to my family.'

Bogue stared intently at him and then beckoned toward Joe. 'What about you?'

'I'm of the same mind as Pete,' Joe replied. 'Whatever he decides, I'm happy with.'

'Don't you have a mind of your own? Don't you have a family that you should be at home with? A pretty girl?' A leer crossed Bogue's face. 'A young feller like you should have plenty of pretty girls ...' He left the sentence hanging in the warm air.

Joe glared at Bogue. 'Pete's as good as my family. I know that he wouldn't do anything to deliberately put me in danger. That's good enough for me.'

Bogue just nodded his head. 'I really don't know what to do with you fellers,' he said in mock exasperation. 'The easy thing would be to shoot you both and leave you for the coyotes.'

Maxwell sniggered.

'You, too,' Bogue said sharply. 'I haven't decided what to do with you yet either.' The smile disappeared from Maxwell's face.

'Let us go home,' Pete said. 'We won't bother you any more.'

Bogue smiled. 'I think we all know that ain't going to happen. You'd probably raise a posse and come charging out here after me, if your pursuit of this bandit who robbed your bank is anything to go by.'

'Well, let us come with you,' Pete said. 'We can help you. The trail is dangerous. It would be safer with us all travelling together.'

'Throw your guns over here,' Bogue said, seemingly ignoring Pete's suggestion.

Pete and Joe loosened their gun belts but Maxwell spoke up. 'Now, just hold on a minute . . .'

Pete's hand flashed to his falling holster, whipped his gun out by the butt and brought the butt down heavily on the back of Maxwell's head.

Maxwell crashed to the ground and his horse snickered.

Bogue's finger hovered over the trigger of his Colt, ready to fire, yet the look in his eyes showed he wasn't sure where to aim. Maxwell had dropped so quickly from his horse that he probably hadn't even seen what hit him.

Pete held his revolver away from his body, the butt between his thumb and forefinger.

'Don't shoot!' he shouted to Bogue. He dropped the gun to the ground. Joe's guns lay on the ground also while Maxwell was obviously unconscious.

'My gut instinct tells me to gun you all down, to end this. To resolve these complications.'

Pete studied his manic expression, the burning eyes and the taut chin. If he didn't break through the murderous haze that seemed to consume Bogue, he'd never see his family again. He shouted, 'We're unarmed. Don't shoot. Let's talk.'

Bogue continued to stare, moving his gun in little jerks between Pete and Joe. He was like a startled animal, threatening to lash out, wanting to vent his frustration through violence.

'You're fast,' he muttered to Pete at

last.

'He was going to get us all killed,' Pete replied. 'I had to do something.'

Saddle leather creaked as Bogue studied them. 'I suppose you fellers might be useful,' he said, finally.

'What about him?' Pete nodded at Maxwell.

'I have my own plans for him,' Bogue replied.

# 13

They moved on, Maxwell thrown across his saddle. Bogue removed their rifles and dismantled all their weapons and threw them into the Platte. *This was becoming a really bizarre assignment*, Bogue thought. He hadn't been in other people's company much since the war ended. He'd become so used to relying on himself that travelling with these fellers unsettled him. His worries were eased somewhat by the fact that he was the only one armed. He could wipe them out whenever he wished. Finding this Maxwell feller should ultimately work in his favour, also. It should allow him to collect his money and escape from the father unharmed. A fair trade. The last surviving son in exchange for the cash he was owed, and maybe a little more. That was what he hoped would happen, anyway.

As for the marshal and deputy? He

wasn't so sure what to do with them. He was convinced that Joe was something of a simpleton, a dog that just followed his master around. He couldn't understand that kind of loyalty. That was totally alien to his way of thinking. Pete Baker was another matter entirely. He now felt a grudging respect for him and his abilities. If he could continue to string him along he might find a use for him. And, failing that, he could always kill him.

* * *

The trail passed in a blur for Pete. His mind worked feverishly, trying desperately to figure out how he could turn this situation back to his advantage. The miles slid by unnoticed. Not a word was spoken amongst the group. He had no idea how this was going to end.

They crossed the South Platte and carried on up the north bank of the Platte's southern arm. After Ash Hollow, they passed some uneventful days before coming to Chimney Rock. The landscape had changed after Ash Hollow, and distinctively shaped rock formations, the product of erosion by wind and rain, loomed ahead. After Chimney Rock, they came to another famous trail landmark, Scott's Bluff. The bluff, yellow clay and soft sand rock, washed and broken into fantastic shapes by wind, rain and storm, presented the appearance of an immense city of towers.

They passed by these sites without remark; only Joe seemed to take time to drink in the stunning scenery. Pete spent his time deep in thought. Thinking of home, of Dorothy, of little Tom. And of how he'd foolishly put himself in such danger. Would he die without ever seeing them again? Would he be buried in some shallow grave or left to rot in the sun? Just another set of bleached bones that dotted the side of the trail? It was his duty to his family to make sure that didn't happen, that he made it home safely so he could support them.

He would have to continue on with

Bogue if he were to have any chance of capturing the bank robber.

Bogue had the upper hand, for now. Pete focused his gaze on the way ahead, determined to stay sharp and alert, and prepared to grasp any opportunity to improve his position should it come along.

\* \* \*

Weston spent the night tossing and turning restlessly on the plain. He didn't know what to do. When Chet found him, he'd been running from death. The same kind of death he himself had dealt out in the Kansas Belle.

He'd been trying to get away from those who wanted to avenge those killings. He was still running from them. At what point would he make a stand? That was what played on his mind, keeping him awake. He felt like he was walking away from his responsibilities, as well as his friends. But, he wondered, was he enough of a man to return to the wagon train and help them out?

He watched the sun rising over the horizon. Slowly, he gathered himself up from the ground and flung his blanket across his horse's back. He saddled and mounted up and turned his horse to face Fort Laramie. He stared hard at the distant fort, thought of what was there, who was there. He thought of Rose.

He had tried to keep her from his thoughts all night. He'd run through every argument for and against returing to the wagon train, tried to be rational and not let his emotions rule. But in the middle of the night he realised that this was futile. He found himself unable to make a decision, something that had never happened to him before. He was a man of action; shoot first and ask questions later. Self-preservation at all costs. He'd always been like that, at least as far back as he could remember. The war had made him that way.

That devastation had taken something from him, stolen a part of him. It was something he no longer acknowledged, so long forgotten that he wasn't sure it had ever existed. But the very thing he feared had happened. And last night just confirmed it. Rose's face had hovered over every thought that entered his head. She'd overridden every argument. Chet had awoken a humanity in him that he'd forgotten he possessed. But Rose had done something more, taken it a step further. And it hurt. She'd reawakened parts of him he thought had died when he saw his parents loading all they had into an open wagon and leaving their home forever.

He'd been living this life for far too long. Always walking in the shadows, always keeping his back to the wall in saloons, his hands all the time ready to drop to his holsters and draw his silver-plated Colts. And for what? What had he to show for it? The final job he'd pulled had been a disaster. He'd tried to become an honest man but the fates had conspired against him. Or, at least, the Maxwells had conspired against him.

He cast his mind back to two weeks

ago, when he discovered he'd been tricked, made to look like a fool. When they had laughed in his face. And then to the brutal retribution he had extracted. His face hardened as he remembered pumping those fellers full of lead. His blood ran quicker as he recalled how he wiped the sneer from Josiah Maxwell's face. Permanently.

He pulled at the reins of his horse and swung around, away from Fort Laramie and all that it held, and rode slowly across the plain. He was going to finish the job he started; otherwise he'd be running for the rest of his life, never safe no matter where he was. He refused to look back at Fort Laramie, not allowing himself to peer over his shoulder until he knew that it was hidden beyond the horizon. As he rode, he slipped back into the solitary ways he'd been used to for so long, the silence, the constant caution, always on edge, waiting for the bullet with his name on it. The wagon train already seemed like a different life, as if it had happened to someone else.

Yet thoughts of the wagoners gradually edged into his mind. Images of Chet and Betty, of Emmet and Angie, of the Butterses and even of the Gileses. But, of course, one image above all stayed before his eyes: Rose. He imagined her every feature, his inner gaze lingering on her eyes, her cheeks, her mouth. He was drawn into this vision of Rose and imagined what he'd say to her if he saw her again. He even began to visualise what a life with her would be like. He was so wrapped up in his thoughts he didn't spot the band of Indians waiting for him on the trail until it was too late.

He reached into his saddle scabbard for his rifle and rested his hand on its stock, ready to pull it free. He recognised a few of the braves' faces. This was the band that had harassed the wagons. Even though he hadn't killed the brave, he had no doubt that if they were in the mood for revenge he'd suit them just fine. They didn't appear aggressive at the moment, however, and that was why he didn't pull out his Winchester. Also, no matter how good a shot he was, he didn't think he could escape unhurt from a group this large. Better to try and talk around this problem, if at all possible.

He'd learned from experience that a lot of the time with Sioux it depended on the impression he gave. Appear capable, able to look after yourself and look like you can fire straight and you had a chance of being left alone. Wander along on your horse like some innocent farmer, daydreaming about your lost love and you'll more than likely find yourself in trouble. He kept his hand on the stock of his rifle, in case the situation changed for the worse.

The chief greeted Weston.

He returned the greeting as the braves spread out around them, encircling them.

Weston scanned their faces, searching for any sign of imminent attack. They looked sternly back at him. There was no mock joviality now, no attempt at trading.

'You leave your friends?' the chief

asked in halting English.

Weston just stared at him, not answering.

'Not safe, travel by yourself. My men very angry.' He swept his hand to encompass his braves.

'That was your own fault,' Weston replied. 'That feller was going to get shot sooner or later, the way he was going.'

A smile crossed the chief's face. He stared hard at Weston. 'You are lost,' he said at last.

Weston glared back at him. 'Not sure what you mean. I know exactly where I'm headed.'

The chief shook his head. 'No. I can see it in your eyes. You're running from something. Or from someone. You are frightened.'

The chief's words burned into Weston like a branding iron. All the thoughts that he'd tried to bury, tried to hide away in some corner of his mind, now returned to the surface. For a moment his gaze wavered and his eyes flicked downward. 'I've seen things, Chief, that no man should have to see.'

'We have all seen things,' the chief replied. 'It is the time we live in.'

'Yes,' Weston said quietly. 'But I have been the cause of many of the terrible scenes I've witnessed.' There was something about the Indian's silence as well as the peacefulness of the plain that compelled Weston to go on, to unburden himself. 'I was part of a massacre, a butchering. It was inhuman.' He wasn't even talking to the chief any more. The words just flowed as if a dam had burst inside of him. 'I was with Quantrill in Lawrence. After we destroyed the place the Union took their revenge. They were determined to drive all the supporters of Quantrill's guerrillas from the area. Some had no wagons and had to travel on foot. Women and children, barefoot and bareheaded, exposed to the heat of an August sun and forced to struggle through the dust . . .

'The road from Independence to Lexington was crowded with women and children, women walking with their babies in their arms, packs on their back, and four or five children following after them — some crying for bread, some crying to be taken back to their homes.

'Those who had wagons headed toward Kansas. Large trains stretched for miles over the prairie, laden down with everything they had left in the world. And behind them their homes burned, smoke rising in every direction. Pretty soon, all that was left were the remains of seared and blackened chimneys. Our farm was one of those that burned. I'd returned home after the Lawrence raid. Thrown myself back into work, farming the land with my father and mother.'

He went quiet once more, thinking back to his upbringing. He was an only child, a product of his and his family's circumstances. They'd arrived in the country in the 1840s from Ireland along with so many of their compatriots, leaving behind hardship in hope of a better life, accepting the loss of their former lives, the forced abandonment of everything that they'd known.

The violent ripping of the umbilical cord that connected them to their home sod could have ruined them. Could have caused them to become destitute and wallow in the warm, comfortable, dissolute poverty of the Five Points. But Charlie's father was of stronger stock and had greater ambitions. He wasn't going to let the unfamiliarity of his new country deter him from making a new life for his family. He wasn't going to let the horror, the baseness, the disease, the darkness, the stench, the vomit, the filth and waste, the overwhelming dehumanisation of the crossing in the belly of a creaking hulk — a contemporary reliving of the journey of the ebony slaves from Africa, ripped from their womb and excreted onto a quayside to be absorbed into this great country — prevent him from grinding out a life, from working for his son and wife.

They crossed in the filth of steerage, a boat for cattle. And then endured the terror of the Immigration officers, who would or wouldn't allow them to be

Americans — the woman next to him with milky eyes not getting in, staying on the island, in seclusion. In America but not in America.

'My father was a great man,' Charlie continued, 'and I let him down. He had to leave his home once; to do so a second time ripped his soul from his body. And because of me that happened. Because I followed Quantrill, we were thrown off our farm. Turned out of our homes. But he never reproached me. I never caught him staring accusingly at me. But because my actions had directly led to our eviction, I knew that I'd just about killed my father.'

'You are carrying a lot of pain,' the chief replied. 'You should go back to your friends. There is only death down this road,' he said, pointing eastward. 'Come with us to Fort Laramie.'

Weston stared at him yet saw nothing but the image of Rose's face before his eyes. He was angry too. Angry with the chief for dredging up those memories, angry with himself for not noticing the Sioux on the trail, angry with Rose for making such an impression on him, but most of all angry with the world for taunting him so cruelly.

There was no way he could go back; no way that she could want him. No way that she could desire him as badly as he wanted her. This fear of opening himself up, of allowing another person into his life was what really terrified him. He'd loved nobody but his parents, and the thought of what happened to them, and of the pain it caused him when they died always rode roughshod over any other emotions he might feel for other people. And he'd killed many people, both during the war and after. This was a cruel, tough world. And fellers like him only made it crueller and tougher.

He was sure that he had slain the loved ones of many people in his time. And the thought of someone like himself coming along and killing Rose, taking her away from him just like that, was too much for him to bear. He could only bring danger to her. He dug his spurs into his horse's flanks and surged forward, pushing past the chief and through the braves that surrounded him.

The chief put up his hand to signal to let him go and they watched as he moved off down the trail. The Sioux moved on, headed for Fort Laramie.

After about ten minutes there was a call from the rear of the group. The chief spun around and gazed back down the trail. Slowly but surely a figure on horseback drew closer. They waited for him and when Charlie Weston joined them they closed around him and continued on their way to Fort Laramie.

When they rode into the fort there were a few comments about the white man riding with the Sioux. But not many.

The rules were different out here. Indeed, many said there were no rules.

Weston thanked the Sioux chief with a nod of his head. No more words were needed.

Then he set to finding out about the train and its whereabouts, and he soon discovered that they'd left. Not a major surprise. He'd expected it, but had secretly hoped that he would have found Rose waiting for him at the fort. But why would she? The uncertainties that had driven him away the first time began to resurface once more, but he pushed them back down.

Despite his outward demeanour, his aggression and decisiveness, he harboured a deep-seated insecurity. He didn't choose his solitary existence; circumstances had contrived to make it so. Meeting Rose had rekindled memories of a life forgotten, a life torn from him by the war. Now he had to take the opportunity to seize it again.

He had to work fast. He was aware that the next stage of the trail was arduous, and could be the biggest test for the wagon train. He must get some supplies and set out after Rose.

★ ★ ★

The next leg was a difficult one for the wagoners with some gruelling terrain to be negotiated before they reached Fort Bridger, just another way station, another sparse fort in the nothingness.

After they left Fort Laramie, they headed through the Red Buttes toward the north fork of the Platte. Many of them were in sullen, wilful or even mutinous mood, unwilling to take orders, nitpicking, and arguing about every single issue: where to cross, who should go first, whether it was fair to ask the column to look after its weakest members. Overall, a nasty, selfish, cynical mood had developed, making life increasingly difficult for Emmet McCann. He missed the forceful presence of Charlie Weston.

Perhaps the absence of timber and kindling contributed to the generally sour mood in the caravan, for west of Fort Laramie they could no longer rely on buffalo chips for fuel but had to forage for scarce scrub lumber. On the other hand, the absence of Indians encouraged them, for this was sparsely populated terrain.

At all events, the journey to the farewell point of the Platte was uneventful. The travellers reached the north fork and began to ford the river by hauling wagons across with ropes. The cow column crossed first, followed by the rest. The north fork was notoriously treacherous, with deceptively swift currents at play even when it was shallow.

Rose continued on implacably, doing her best to involve herself in the goings-on of the train but all the while feeling strangely detached. She couldn't shake the heaviness that had descended on her nor rouse herself from the torpor it brought with it. Something had changed within her, and it wasn't because of the weather or diet or the leaving of Fort Laramie. It was because of who had left her.

All day and all night she thought constantly of Weston, and cursed him for what he had done to her. He'd made her doubt herself, had made her look at the life she was living and she didn't like what she saw. But she no longer had any choice. She was in the foothills of the Rocky Mountains and heading west. This was now her life.

The last week in July saw the emigrants finally clear of the prairie and climbing upward. The landscape had changed, becoming more barren and forbidding, the hills blue-grey and the vegetation mainly sagebrush, with here and there the odd dwarf cedar. This was desolate country where the few waterholes were so adulterated with salt that even the animals refused to drink. Although the pioneers had encountered alkali-infested pools along the Platte valley, there'd always been clean, fresh water nearby. But now, as they cut further across country to the Sweetwater, they were assailed by the spectre of disease. 'Mountain fever' lurked in the air, threatening to cut down anybody who was less than vigilant with their hygiene.

The inroads of disease were fortunately curtailed as they progressed to higher and higher altitudes, where nights were cold, with severe frosts and water freezing in the kettles; once darkness fell, many of the travellers huddled over stoves with their overcoats on. For the few who had leisure enough to appreciate the picturesque, the Wind River Range made an impressive snow-covered backdrop.

After Independence Rock, the next significant landmark along the Sweetwater was Devil's Gate, a massive granite formation of almost perpendicular rock where the river ran through a narrow chasm, forcing the rock to tower three hundred feet above the water.

They came to the Continental Divide at South Pass, and camped for the night. A horseman appeared on the trail behind them. They watched him draw closer, his mount moving slowly but purposefully, closing the gap between them. Chet and Emmet made their way back to the wagons and drew out their rifles.

Morale was low and any outsider was viewed as a danger or an enemy. The figure grew larger against the hills behind. They readied their weapons, just in case. They watched him come closer, their fingers tightening, as did their nerves. They were still debating what to do when a figure rushed across their line of vision, hurtling down the trail toward the lone rider.

'What. . . ?' McCann spluttered.

'That's Rose,' Chet murmured in amazement.

★ ★ ★

She felt as if her heart were about to burst. When she'd seen him approaching, she knew immediately that it was Weston. She'd tried to stay where she was, tried to watch dispassionately as he rode closer. Exasperatingly, it seemed to her that he was barely moving. Eventually, it was as though she lost control of her own body. Before she knew it, she found herself running to him. She saw nothing but Weston, nothing but his strong silhouette against the darkening sky.

She ran faster than she even knew she could. She didn't reason that he might be there for some reason other than for her; that was not a thought worth contemplating. He was back for her, it was as simple as that.

He slipped down the side of his horse and as soon as his feet hit the ground he ran toward her.

They embraced, almost falling over in their excitement.

Rose sobbed with happiness.

Emotion flowed through Weston; he was overwhelmed by the flood of love he had been keeping at bay for so long.

They held each other tight, oblivious to their surroundings and the eyes that watched them, cocooned in their own private world.

★ ★ ★

All the attention that night was on Weston.

'What made you come back?' Chet asked mischievously.

Emmet glared at him but was unable to keep the smile from his lips. His daughter was happy, that was all that mattered to him. They could work out matters in more detail when they eventually reached their destination.

'I just missed all you folks so much,' Weston said.

They all laughed. Rose sat next to him, huddled against him.

'You coming all the way with us?' Butters asked.

'If that's all right with you?' Weston asked of Emmet.

'You're more than welcome,' he replied. Emmet extended his hand and they shook firmly.

Weston nodded in gratitude, unable to articulate the appreciation he felt. Emmet could have told him to clear out, to hightail it back to Fort Laramie, and maybe even sent a volley of lead after him, for what he'd done to Rose. This was a chance for Weston to make a new life now. But first they had to make it safely to California.

Rose clung to Weston that night, afraid that if she let go of him he might disappear again. Eventually, at some hour of the morning as they both lay awake under the stars, she asked him all the questions she'd wanted to ask. She asked him about himself. Her words seemed to drift off into the prairie sky but Weston heard them all right and waited for a long time before he answered.

She was afraid that she'd said something to anger him but all of a sudden the words began to flow. He told her of Quantrill, of the raid on Lawrence in 1863. Of what the raid had done to him — of the Charlie Weston before Rose had come along. He told her about the devastation caused by the Lawrence massacre and the terrible havoc wreaked on his parents and their neighbours as retribution. And about how he felt as if his hands were stained with the blood of the innocents and with the tears of his parents.

'I headed west after that,' he said, 'and vowed never to return home again. I joined a gang of bandits and put myself in the way of danger almost every day of my life, not really caring if I lived or died. Until one day I finally had enough. I was going to pull off one big job and then see about buying some land and settling down. Try to recreate the life taken from my parents. Maybe I'd find some peace of mind that way. But the fates had a trick up their sleeves for me. Deep down, I wasn't really surprised when Josiah Maxwell tricked me out of my money when he sold me falsified land certificates.

'But I had his revenge, gunned him down in the Kansas Belle. That would surely bring about the end, my life would soon be over, I thought. But, instead, it brought me you.'

They held each other tightly, that night, keeping the cold at bay. Rose eventually slipped off to sleep in his arms. When she woke the next morning, he was still awake, gazing at her.

The wagons rolled out soon after.

It wasn't long before they reached Pacific Springs. From there they pro-ceeded southeast across rough, arid country, fording the Little Sandy and the other streams of Sandy Creek, until they reached the rapid-flowing Green River, broad and beautiful, pursuing its long course through Wyoming, Flaming Gorge and Colorado before finally debouching into the Colorado River and southeast Utah.

After a halt at the Green River, they continued in a southwesterly direction, over Ham's Fork, a major tributary of the Green, then rumbled south of and parallel to Black's Fork, making for Fort Bridger. They soon found themselves in a wasteland as grim, arid and barren as any they had encountered, tormented by mirages, which the animals apparently also saw and were maddened by.

Trekking in poor visibility through whorls of dust, the wagoners suffered grievously from billowing sand and intense heat. The wagons creaked from cracking hubs and loosened tyres. They were caught between the perils of the desert, pressing down on the parched and plodding oxen with pulverised particles of sand, and the dangers of the mountain, whose arid atmosphere caused all iron tyres on wood that wasn't properly seasoned to work loose.

Some of the travellers tried driving wedges between the tyre and the wheel but there was neither time nor opportunity to try the usual remedy of removing the wheel and soaking it in a stream overnight. There was nothing for it but to hold on grimly and await the blacksmith's shop at Fort Bridger.

But, unbeknownst to them, their slowing progress was providing an opportunity for their pursuers to catch up with them.

# 14

The four men dismounted just inside the gates of the fort. An air of unease and apprehension hung over them, as if their edgy alliance was drawing to a close. It was immediately obvious to them that there were no wagon trains at the fort. They'd already left, a fact that didn't improve Bogue's mood. 'I'd have been quicker without you jiggers,' he shouted at his prisoners. 'I should've shot you out on the prairie.'

They remained silent. They were weary, drained by the hard pace they had set the last few days. This wasn't the first time that Bogue had lost his temper and threatened to kill them. His threats were becoming wearisome and Pete hardly even heard them any more. He ached all over. Bogue had tied them all together at night, bound hand and foot, which didn't make for comfortable sleeping. To make matters worse, it seemed as if

Bogue never closed his eyes and never slept. He just sat watching them all night. This may have aggravated his ever darkening mood and Pete sensed that, one way or the other, the end was near.

'Stay here,' Bogue said, 'I'm going to find out when they left.'

'How's about you let us help you out?' Pete asked. 'The sooner we find out what's happening, the sooner we'll be on our way.'

Bogue looked doubtfully at him.

'Come on, Joe,' Pete said, 'let's have a look around. If he shoots us here, he'll just be arrested and that's not what he wants.'

Bogue glared at him for a long moment. 'Back here in thirty minutes, OK?' Bogue said through gritted teeth.

'See you then,' Pete replied. They walked away from Bogue and Maxwell.

'You trying to get us killed?' Joe asked.

'He wouldn't dare kill us here,' Pete replied.

'Sure, but what about when we leave the fort? Why don't we just leave him, make a break for it?' Joe continued.

Pete stared at his companion and saw something in his eyes. It wasn't fear but it wasn't complete trust, either. Pete felt bad. He knew that Joe would do whatever he asked him but he also knew that he was now putting him in more danger than he ever had before. Even though Joe was his own man and wouldn't do anything he felt wasn't right, Pete's influence and opinion meant a lot to him.

Pete also felt guilty because, deep down, he knew that his motivations were basically selfish. He was rediscovering his own self-worth on this journey. The chase after the bank robber had become personal, a battle of wits and minds. Their capture by Bogue only accentuated the challenge, sharpening his senses and his instincts. If he could only survive this, if he could only take the bank robber back to Baxter Springs, he knew that his life would be better. For both him and his family.

But it was different for Joe, he knew. 'If you want to leave, Joe, I'll help you get away. I mean that. This is my battle. I'm not sure that I could ever forgive myself if you got killed out here.'

Joe stared at his friend, his colleague, the man with whom he'd been through many scrapes. 'If you're staying, I'm staying.'

'If I got back without you, Dorothy would kill me anyway.' Pete smiled.

'Seeing as we're sticking around, we might as well work out what we plan on doing,' Joe said.

They were in a strange situation. They had gathered from Bogue that they were chasing a wagon train and that Bogue had been paid to kill someone on that train. Also, Maxwell was in on it somehow. That was all they knew at present. Pete just hoped that they were after the same man and now was as good a time as any to find out.

Pete learned from asking around Fort Laramie that the wagon train had been and left, 'maybe a couple of days ago, maybe more'. When he and Joe met up with Bogue and Maxwell the mules had been restocked with fresh supplies of water and food.

'Your daddy better give me some more money when this is over and done with,' Bogue said to Maxwell. 'I'm spending a whole lot on this job of his.'

'Don't you worry,' Maxwell sneered, 'I'm sure he'll be mighty generous once you do what you're supposed to do.'

An hour later, they rode out through the gates and rejoined the trail heading west.

'Who are you after anyway?' Pete asked Bogue. 'You know all our stories, how about you share a little? Maybe we can help? You too, Maxwell. You're a mighty mysterious character. You say he's working for your daddy but he's treating you like some sort of prisoner.'

Maxwell turned and glared at him. 'Don't you worry about me, feller. I'm pretty sure that I'll be just fine.'

Bogue sniggered. 'You fellers are like a bunch of hens, pecking at each other.'

'I meant what I said; maybe Joe and I can help.'

'Maybe . . .' Bogue muttered.

'Who are you after?' Pete asked. 'Who are you going to kill?'

Bogue sneered. All these questions. He was beginning to think that the only way to get some peace and quiet was to kill these fellers and be done with it. But something Pete had said struck a chord, had maybe offered him a solution to a problem that lurked at the back of his mind. No matter which way he looked at it, the wagon train would have plenty of men and plenty of guns. Even though he was confident he could take down most of them, there was the possibility that Weston might slip away in the commotion, or maybe that Maxwell might get killed, which would also complicate matters.

If Weston caught sight of him, he'd know he was there to kill him. And he'd fight back. In fact, Weston would shoot the moment he saw Bogue, before his brain even had a chance to process the information it received from his eyes. It was sheer animal instinct. The exact same thing Bogue would do in the same situation. 'I'm after Charlie Weston,' he said to Pete.

Air whistled through Pete's teeth. Charlie Weston. He rolled the name around in his head. Bogue and Weston, two of the fiercest gunfighters going up against each other. It could only lead to carnage and bloodshed.

'Is he the feller that robbed the bank?' Bogue nodded.

'What's he doing out here, then? This doesn't make a whole lot of sense to me.'

'I think our friend here can tell you more about that than I can,' Bogue said as he stared at Maxwell.

'Don't know what you're talking about,' Maxwell said gruffly.

'Come on,' Bogue said, 'what scam did your father and brother pull on him? I know Charlie Weston and he's no angel, but he wouldn't just break loose like that for no reason. I've got a feeling that the money Weston stole from that bank might be paying my fee. At least a bit of it, anyway.' He left the thought hanging in the air.

Pete looked sideways at Maxwell, who had clammed up completely.

They rode on, chasing the wagons, making ground rapidly as the train limped along ahead of them. Night began to fall but still Bogue kept them moving. It was as if he could smell his quarry up ahead, ready for the taking.

At last, the fires from the camp could be seen, illuminating a small patch of sky above where the wagoners had settled for the night.

Bogue gestured to the others to be silent and they steadied their pace, proceeding more carefully now. They halted behind a large bluff.

The emigrants were camped less than a quarter of a mile away.

# 15

Pete set off from their hiding place alone, making for the wagons. He wasn't happy with the arrangement that Bogue had dictated but he hadn't had much choice in the matter. Joe was back behind the bluff with Bogue and Maxwell, a gun levelled at his chest and ready to go off should Pete not carry out his instructions correctly. Bogue had told him to go into camp and have a look around, come up with some story and slip away back during the night with all his information. Pete crossed the distance slowly but deliberately, giving himself a chance to think while not making Bogue suspicious.

Bogue had given him a gun, but he could tell from its weight that it wasn't loaded. It was purely for show. He knew that the ideal scenario for Bogue would be for Pete to arrest Weston and bring him right to him. That would make

Bogue's life very easy and surely sign Joe and Pete's death warrants. No, he had to come up with something before he met Charlie Weston. He had the horrible feeling that the very man he had chased for so long, was so determined to arrest and bring to justice, might just be the only man who could help him get back safely to his family.

Pete emerged out of the gloom and was at the edge of the camp before he was even noticed. 'Howdy,' he said loudly, making sure that he announced himself before any lead started flying in his direction.

The men all jumped to their feet but Pete put his arms out from his sides to indicate that he wasn't a threat. 'You fellers didn't post any sentries tonight,' he said. 'You're lucky I'm not some outlaw.'

'That remains to be seen,' someone muttered.

'We were exhausted,' another voice called. 'Had trouble with wagon wheels. Maybe you could help us out in the morning, get us back under way?'

'Maybe,' Pete said quietly. He had no intention of being around in the morning.

'What's your story, stranger?'

'Heading from Fort Laramie to Fort Bridger, carrying messages.' As he spoke, he scanned the camp in the half-light until his eyes settled on the man Bogue had described: Charlie Weston.

Weston stood in front of a pretty young girl, obviously protecting her from whatever danger he felt Pete had brought. Weston's eyes didn't carry the cold, emotionless blankness that he'd seen in so many killers, he thought. This man seemed like any other. Sure, he looked tough, but there was an openness about his face. This gave Pete some hope; maybe he'd be able to rely on him for help, after all.

'Why don't you camp with us for the night?' a voice suggested.

'Much obliged,' Pete replied, 'and I'll help you out in the morning.'

Later, Pete waited for the sounds of the camp to settle down before making his move. He raised himself up on one elbow and listened intently. All seemed quiet. He was just about to get to his feet when he heard a noise behind him before feeling the cold steel of the gun barrel pressed against his cheek. He looked up at Charlie Weston.

Weston gestured to Pete to get up and walk. They left the camp and when Weston felt they were a safe distance away, he shoved Pete to the ground. Pete fell heavily. Weston whipped Pete's pistol out of its holster.

'Why's your gun empty?' Weston asked, bemused. 'You're trouble. I could tell from the moment you arrived. I should drill you right now and save myself a problem down the line.'

Pete held his gaze. His threats sounded much like Bogue's but there was something different about Weston. He didn't possess that closed nature that enveloped Bogue; there was humanity behind his eyes. 'You'd better tell me right now who you are or I'm going to start getting real angry.'

'Name's Pete Baker, marshal of Baxter Springs.'

This made Weston start. 'Baxter Springs?' he exclaimed. 'You the feller tried to stop me getting away with the money?' He shook his head in confusion. 'You come all the way out here to arrest me or something?'

Pete heard the shock in Weston's voice. He really couldn't believe that he'd trailed him all this way. He thought about what to say next. Yes, his original intention had been to arrest Weston, but that was before the game changed. He decided to come clean and tell Weston everything about Bogue and Maxwell.

When Pete stopped talking, Weston lowered his gun. 'I should've known Maxwell wouldn't give up,' he said wistfully. 'What do you propose?' he asked Pete.

\* \* \*

Bogue saw two figures approaching from the direction of the camp, backlit by the dawn sky. He recognised them immediately. Charlie Weston, arms upraised with Pete's gun jammed into his back. Bogue, unable to contain himself, turned to Joe. 'Your friend's done good,' he sneered.

Bogue lost interest in Joe and Maxwell as he impatiently watched the two figures approaching from around the side of the bluff. As they drew near, Bogue stepped out and made himself known. 'Charlie Weston,' he said. 'You've been worth the hunt.'

Bogue's hands dropped to his sides and drew his Colts. He fired fast at Weston, aiming to kill him on the spot.

Weston had been expecting Bogue's deadly move. He knew that if he were in Bogue's position he would have done the same thing.

He dove to his side and knocked Pete to safety. Even so, a bullet carried most of Pete's shirtsleeve with it, drawing blood from his forearm. Weston had barely hit the ground when he was firing at Bogue, forcing him to dive back behind the bluff for cover. If Bogue hadn't been so preoccupied with Weston, he might have noticed that both Joe and Maxwell had disappeared, hightailing toward the camp.

Bogue cursed. He should have shot Weston immediately. He shouldn't have indulged in gloating for those few seconds. It was just that he couldn't help himself. He'd felt so happy, so satisfied. He just had to make sure now that he finished the job.

Weston barked at Pete to follow him. They dashed, hunched over, for the cover of a low rocky embankment. They were followed by bullets eating up the ground at their feet. As they collapsed behind their cover, Weston said breathlessly, 'Leave Bogue to me. I want you to go back to the camp and watch after Rose. Keep her safe. She's all I've got.'

Pete was about to protest and insist that he help fight against Bogue when Weston charged from his cover and ran in the direction of the bluff, all the while firing to keep Bogue ducking behind his cover.

Then Weston's gun hammer struck the empty cylinder.

Grinning broadly, Bogue emerged from around the bluff. Weston launched himself through the air and tackled him to the ground.

★　★　★

Joe and Maxwell ran at full pelt toward the camp. Joe had seen Pete and Weston crouched behind their cover but without any weapon he figured that he wouldn't be of any use to them. Best to head for the wagons and muster up some support there, he decided. Once there, they were greeted by the business ends of rifles and revolvers as they almost collapsed after their frantic dash.

'Stop right there,' barked a clearly shaken man. 'What in hell is going on?' he seemed to ask nobody in particular.

Between gulping breaths, Joe spoke fast, explaining the situation.

Rose let out a pained cry when she heard that Weston was in grave danger.

She collapsed to the ground and her mother comforted her.

'Well, let's go help Charlie,' Chet said as soon as Joe finished. He tossed both Joe and Maxwell a gun. There were now five of them bearing weapons: Emmet, Chet, Butters, Joe and Maxwell, and they ran off toward the fight.

* * *

Weston set upon Bogue with a savage intensity, lashing at him with his arms, his legs, his empty gun, anything that he could use as a weapon. Bogue seemed taken by surprise by the sudden attack. He fell to the ground under the weight of Weston's charge, his guns spilling from his hands. He used his arms to absorb as much of Weston's frantic blows as possible. Weston struck with a ferocity that was born from his determination to preserve this new life that he had found.

He wasn't perfect. He'd killed people, but Rose loved him, which meant that he had to be worth something. The war had changed so many men. Made good men do things that they'd have nightmares about for the rest of their lives. It was a black cloud that hung over their young country's history, blighting a generation. But now Weston had seen that there was another way. He could break free from the destructive cycle he'd found himself in. He must put Bogue out of action. The blood of one more man was the price he would have to pay.

Bogue regained his poise and saw an opportunity. He obviously sensed that Weston was tiring and he lashed out at his face. There was the familiar crunch of fist against bone and cartilage.

Weston paused, stunned for a moment, and Bogue took his chance. He kicked Weston off him and got to his feet before landing a couple more heavy blows.

Weston staggered, disorientated, and watched hazily as Bogue made for one of his guns on the ground. Desperately, ignoring the searing pain in his face, Weston lunged forward once more and locked his arms round Bogue's knees, knocking him to the ground. He took two swift kicks to the side of his face for his efforts, however, and once again Bogue broke free.

Bogue scrambled over the dry earth and fell on his Colt.

Weston half ran, half crawled after him, fists clenched and ready for more action, before he was stopped dead in his tracks by the barrel of Bogue's gun thrust into his face.

'This is it, Weston! No more messing around,' Bogue growled.

Though the gun barrel was directly in front of his face, all Weston thought about was Rose. Her beauty filled his mind as he heard the weapon go off.

Gun-smoke clouded his vision. There was a heavy thud as the body hit the ground, a hole in his shirt where the bullet had entered. Though Weston's eyes were open, he still hadn't seen or realised what had happened. When Pete grasped him by the shoulder, he realised that he was still alive, still breathing.

'I got him,' Pete said simply, smoke

drifting from the barrel of Bogue's other Colt.

Weston stared at him blankly, not understanding for a moment.

Pete stretched out his hand and Weston took it, allowing himself to be pulled up off the ground. 'Let's get back to the wagons,' he said.

Weston nodded.

After a few paces, Weston stopped Pete and put a hand on his shoulder. 'Thanks,' he said.

'Any time.' Pete saw the emotion in his eyes and he recognised what Weston was feeling. Weston now had something to live for. He now had a fear of death, and even though that was going to stay with him for the rest of his life, he'd be a better man for it. He would appreciate those around him even more. Just like me, Pete thought.

As they walked back to the wagons they met the others running up.

'You missed the party,' Pete said drolly.

Joe looked at Weston's battered, bruised and bloodied face. 'Looks like it was one hell of a shindig.'

Weston and Pete just smiled in response and continued walking.

Weston was smothered by Rose's hugs when he returned to her. She had convinced herself that he had been taken from her and now his return seemed miraculous. They held each other for a long time and Weston promised never to leave her again. She replied with her tears.

\* \* \*

'I get the feeling we ain't going to be arresting this feller,' Joe said to Pete later that day as they ate their lunch.

'You feel right,' Pete replied. 'I never really enjoyed being marshal anyway.'

'What about the family, the farm? You'll end up in that saloon for the rest of your life.'

Pete nodded glumly. A shadow passed behind them and Pete looked up to see Weston standing over them.

'I can't thank you enough,' he said.

'No problem,' Pete replied.

'I know that by not bringing me back, things might get a bit awkward for you.'

A wry smile crossed Pete's face.

'You could say that.'

'Well, I want to help you out a little.' Weston held the pouch that he'd kept so close to him since the day Chet Harrington had picked him up off the prairie. 'Take it,' he said, handing it to Pete. 'It's what's left of the money. It's for you.'

Pete looked at it dubiously for a while before taking it. He had chased the money and the man across the trail for days and now it appeared that he had both within arm's reach.

'Thanks,' he said, echoing Weston's words when he had saved his life, 'but I'm not sure I can do that. The money belongs to the bank, to the citizens. I'll take it from you but I'll have to give it back. It's what I came for, some of it anyway,' he added with a wry smile.

Joe and Pete left the emigrants the next morning. Maxwell travelled with them but kept to himself. They set a fast but steady pace, each mile they clocked up bringing Pete closer to his family.

'You know something?' Maxwell said eventually. 'I know a nice piece of land you could buy with that money.'

We do hope that you have enjoyed reading this large print book.

Did you know that all of our titles are available for purchase?

We publish a wide range of high quality large print books including:
**Romances, Mysteries, Classics**
**General Fiction**
**Non Fiction and Westerns**

Special interest titles available in large print are:
**The Little Oxford Dictionary**
**Music Book, Song Book**
**Hymn Book, Service Book**

Also available from us courtesy of Oxford University Press:
**Young Readers' Dictionary**
**(large print edition)**
**Young Readers' Thesaurus**
**(large print edition)**

For further information or a free brochure, please contact us at:
**Ulverscroft Large Print Books Ltd.,**
**The Green, Bradgate Road, Anstey,**
**Leicester, LE7 7FU, England.**
**Tel:** (00 44) 0116 236 4325
**Fax:** (00 44) 0116 234 0205

*Other titles in the
Linford Western Library:*

# RED DIAMOND RUSTLERS

## Will DuRey

Law is rare on the vast cattle ranges, and a man must fight if he means to hold on to what he owns. A rancher dispenses his own justice when he catches those who steal his live-stock — but Titus Sawyer lost more than cattle when rustlers raided the Red Diamond. Men were killed too, slaughtered in a dreadful ambush. So when he summoned his nephew Frank to track down the killers, his desire was for something deeper than justice — revenge . . .

# WANTED DEAD OR ALIVE

## Ralph Hayes

A year after being saved from a kidnapping, Dulcie Provost is waiting for the return of her rescuer, bounty hunter Certainty Sumner. But first Sumner has to carry out one more mission — tracking down sadistic outlaw the Lakota Kid. Unbeknownst to Sumner, he himself is also the quarry of an equally ruthless bounty hunter, Luther Bastian. The father of a gang member Sumner killed while rescuing Provost wants vengeance — and has duped Bastian into believing that Sumner has turned outlaw . . .

# MONEY TRAIN

## Michael Stewart

Danny Spence plans to stay only one night in Gila Creek. But he's mistaken for a snake named Zeke Tolan, and from then on it's just one damn thing after another. He falls foul of the evil Ma Cole, then gets on the wrong side of Hernando Ortiz and his sadistic bodyguard Bracho. Somehow, this is all wrapped up with a train full of money that's rolling south of the border — right into the middle of the Mexican revolution.